# Richard
# Victorious

Other books by this author

*Fascinating Foremothers*
*Parents, Poems, and Roots*

# Richard Victorious

SHIRLEY HALL

ISBN: 978-0-244-68484-6


PublishNation
www.publishnation.co.uk

# 1

Richard led the charge. The thunder of hooves and the cries of men in battle all around him as he swung his battle axe and cut down all in his path until the terrified, shrinking face of Henry Tudor was before him. Hesitating for only a second, he swung his axe for one last time and brought it down, splitting Tudor's head from his body with one violent blow.

Richard slumped in the saddle as he slowly removed his helmet and was momentarily dazzled by the sun's rays as it glinted on the edges of the golden crown encircling it. His face, hair, and whole body drenched in sweat, he leaned forward to pat and calm his great war horse, White Surrey, who like his master was be-splattered with the blood and filth of battle. Richard raised his head, shaking his wet hair from his eyes and looked around him at the scene of utter devastation.

'Dickon, Dickon, you have done it.' A rider clamped his mailed hand onto Richard's shoulder as he looked up into the grinning face of his oldest and most trusted friend, Francis, Viscount Lovell.

'Aye, I suppose I have.' He suddenly became aware of the cheers increasing in volume as the word spread like wildfire through the ranks of Richard's army that Henry Tudor was dead and was no longer the Lancastrian threat to the throne.

John Howard, duke of Norfolk was next to reach his king. 'We have them alive, your grace.'

'Who?'

'Them bloody traitors, the Stanley brothers.' Norfolk panted, grasping his left arm as blood oozed down it from a shoulder injury.

'If Northumberland and his men hadn't cut across William Stanley's charge towards you, Sire, as you were within touch of Tudor, today's outcome would have been very different.'

'You are right as usual, Jack,' Richard agreed. 'Although Northumberland was behaving earlier in his usual cautious manner, he came right in the end.' Richard nodded. 'You are bleeding badly, Jack, go and get it attended to, we will talk later.'

'Jasper Tudor is also slain,' Lovell interjected.

'What of de Vere?' Richard asked. 'I want him taken alive.'

John de Vere, the earl of Oxford, was a noted Lancastrian general who had commanded the vanguard of Tudor's army which by now was fleeing the field, casting aside their weapons in their haste to escape the Yorkist victors.

'We do not know de Vere's whereabouts yet, Sire, but he cannot have got very far. He will not escape us.'

Richard nodded wearily. Now that the adrenalin rush caused by battle culminating in the Yorkist victory began to fade, Richard realised that his body ached all over and that the pain in his curved spine from the scoliosis that had plagued him from his early teens, was almost unbearable.

'Someone bring me a drink,' he ordered a squire who ran to a nearby well and returned with a goblet overflowing with cold, clear water.

'Thank you, lad.' Richard drank deeply then tossed the goblet back to the squire who caught it neatly.

'What now, Dickon?' asked Lovell, with the familiarity of an old friend.

'Why, Frank,' the king replied replacing his helmet upon his head. Return to Leicester, of course.'


Richard led his triumphant army back into Leicester. Word of his victory had reached the town before their arrival and they were met by the sounds of church bells and cheering crowds. He had just crossed Bow Bridge when a young girl risking injury from White Surrey's flailing hooves, ran up to him and with a clumsy curtsey, held out a long stemmed white rose. Richard leaned forward and with his quiet smile, took the rose and tucked it into his sword belt.

The girl, aged no more than twelve or thirteen, blushing deeply ran back to where an older woman stood on the edge of the crowd.

'Oh Mother' she cried, ' The king smiled at me. Isn't he lovely?'

'Yes' the mother agreed. 'King Richard is a nice enough looking man but he is nothing like his brother, ah! The tall golden haired king Edward. *Now* he really looked like a king'

What the woman said about the late king Edward was very true. He had stood six foot four inches in height and with his handsome golden looks he would have still attracted the hordes of women with whom he had surrounded himself with even if he hadn't been a king. Richard's appearance was quite different from that of his flamboyant eldest brother. Slim featured with shoulder length hair that had been blond as a child, but it had darkened with maturity to a mid-brown. His eyes blue-grey. He was a slightly built man of five feet eight inches, nothing like King Edward but still a handsome young man of thirty two.

Bringing up the rear of the procession were two carts. The first one containing the manacled figures of Thomas, Lord Stanley and his brother, Sir William Stanley and the newly captured John de Vere, earl of Oxford. Oxford who lay slumped in the cart, injured as he had tried to escape the avenging Yorkist's, with blood streaming from a gashed cheek. The second cart contained the remains of Henry and of Jasper Tudor with a blood soaked Red Dragon standard thrown over them. The bodies were bound for the Market Place where they would remain on public display for two days before their burial in the church of the Grey Friars by order of the king.

Turning into the high Street, Richard dismounted outside the White Boar Inn, Leicester's finest hostelry. He turned to acknowledge the cheers, handed his horse's reins to a waiting groom then entered the building and made his way to the room he had occupied two days earlier. He was met at the door by his grinning body servant, Tom Murgatroyd who dropped awkwardly to his knees grasping his king's hand and kissing it.

'Get up, Tom, get up' said Richard with a laugh. 'There is no need for that.'

Yorkshireman Tom had served Richard from the first day of his arrival as an apprehensive twelve year old at Middleham Castle in Wensleydale. stronghold of his cousin, Richard Neville, earl of Warwick, known as 'the kingmaker' where he was to begin his knightly training. Tom was ten years older than his young master and walked with a slight limp caused by his clubbed left foot.

' I ' ave everything ready fer you, your grac' murmured Tom in his broad Yorkshire accent as he took the helmet from Richard's outstretched hands and placed it on the nearby table. Two Esquires who had followed the king into the room, quickly relieved him of his armour and then at a nod from Richard, bowed and backed out of the room.

'Let me rub thee down wi this 'ere towel then I'll 'elp thee on wi some clean clothes.'

Richard nodded wearily and gladly allowed Tom to sponge his upper body and to dry him with a warm towel before dressing in a blue velvet doublet and matching hose. He then added his customary rings to his long slender fingers before combing his tangled hair. He walked slowly to the chair at the head of the table and winced as he sat down.

'Is it reet bad, Sire?' Tom asked softly. 'I've put an 'ot brick inside of yon cushion. I ope it gives thee some relief'

'Thank you, Tom,' Richard replied as he eased the warm cushion into place on his lower back.

Richard's scoliosis and Tom's club foot combined with the acute discomfort both conditions inflicted had, over the years, formed a special bond of understanding between master and man. Neither of whom would have allowed any public display of pain which would have incurred sympathy, the thought of which would have horrified them. Richard's closest adherents suspected that he often suffered pain but respecting his dignity, never referred to it.

Later in the early evening after the dinner table had been cleared. Richard and his closest friends who had fought beside him at Bosworth, sat at their ease around the fireplace with their tankards of ale and goblets of fine wines. On the King's left lounged Francis Lovell with one leg casually thrown over the arm of his chair. Lovell, one of the wealthiest men in the kingdom, had first met the king at Middleham when they were both being trained in arms, Tall fair haired Francis was two years younger than Richard having been born in 1454, had immediately struck up a friendship that had grown stronger over the years. His father had died when he was only nine years old so at that early age he became the ninth Baron Lovell and the sixth Baron Holland. He was created first Viscount Lovell by Richard in 1483.

The oldest man present at the informal gathering was the sixty four year old Sir Ralph de Assheton, a bluff grizzled warrior from Lancashire where he was Lord of the manor of Ashton – Under – Lyne. He had the well-earned reputation of not being the kind of person to cross, and if you wanted a dirty job doing, he was your man.

In marked contrast was Sir William Catesby. Born in 1450 at Ashby St Ledgers, Northamptonshire. He had trained as a lawyer in the Inner Temple in London and had been in the service of the late William, Lord Hastings before giving his allegiance to Richard then Lord Protector during the brief time following the death of king Edward 1V. Discovering the plot by Lord Hastings and the former Queen Elizabeth Woodville, her relatives and churchmen, John Morton, bishop of Ely and archbishop Rotherham of York. to seize power and depose and probably kill Richard, Catesby sought him out and gave him all the horrific details, thus proving his loyalty and giving Richard the opportunity to thwart their plans by executing Hastings and imprisoning the churchmen. The Queen fled into sanctuary. By his actions, Catesby had become one of Richard's closest Advisors, he held the posts of Chancellor of the Exchequer and Speaker of the House of Commons. A quietly spoken man whose advice Richard greatly valued.

By contrast, sat Sir Robert Percy, belching loudly after swallowing his ale too quickly. Rob, as he was known to all his friends, had been born at Scotton, near Knaresborough in Yorkshire and was a distant relative of the powerful Percy family, earls of Northumberland. A few years older than Richard, whom he also had befriended at Middleham, he was a large powerfully built red haired man with a great sense of humour and a loud hearty laugh which belied his astuteness, A great friend to have at your back in if you ever found yourself in a tight corner.

Sir Richard Ratcliffe, another of Richard's northern friends having been born in the Lake District, sat opposite the king gazing thoughtfully into his loosely held tankard. Ratcliffe, like Lovell and Percy became friends with Richard when growing up together in Middleham. Rewarding Ratcliffe's loyalty, Richard had made him a Knight of the Garter and hereditary High Sheriff of Westmorland.

Suddenly, the door burst open to admit a distraught Thomas Howard, earl of Surrey, eldest son of the Duke of Norfolk.

'Whatever is the matter, Thomas? 'The King asked, amused by Surrey's dramatic entrance. 'Has the inn caught fire?'

'No, your grace' Surrey panted before dropping down onto his knee. ' It is my father, he is dying and begs to see you, Sire' Surrey gasped breathing heavily.

'Dying? I understood his injury was not serious' exclaimed the King.

'He is an old man, Sire, and has lost a lot of blood and now he has suffered some kind of seizure. Please come, Sire before it is too late'

'Show me the way,' said Richard, rising to his feet.

A shocked silence fell as Richard followed Surrey out of the room and up a flight of winding stairs and into a chamber where the only sound was that of Norfolk's laboured breathing. A Priest kneeling at the bedside rose at the king's entrance and withdrew.

Richard was shocked by the change in his old friend's appearance who apart from the wound to his shoulder, had seemed so hearty and well after the battle.

'What's all this lying abed for, Jack?' he asked quietly taking Norfolk's cold hand into his own warm clasp. 'It is not like you to laze around all day'

Norfolk struggled painfully to rise but Richard gently eased him back onto his pillows. ' Nay Jack, I am only jesting, stay where you are for a few days until you are feeling more like yourself again' Norfolk nodded and looked into Richard's eyes and both men knew that that day would never come. Surrey, on the other side of the bed sobbed out his grief as with a long drawn out sigh, John Howard, duke of Norfolk, breathed his last. Richard leant forward and closed his friend's eyes, crossed himself and after laying a comforting hand on Surrey's shoulder, quietly left the room.

The next day dawned without a cloud in the sky with the promise of another perfect summer's day. Just after 10.30 A.M. a sombre king and his closest friends took their places at an upstairs open casement window in the inn. Below them, surrounding the Market Place a company of halberdiers held back the noisy crowds of curious townspeople who had all assembled to witness the executions of the traitors captured following the battle. First to mount the hastily constructed scaffold was John de Vere, 13th earl of Oxford and veteran of numerous Lancastrian campaigns. He mounted casually as if on an ordinary morning stroll. Before kneeling at the block, he turned towards Richard and bowed mockingly to him, then knelt and cried to the Headsman, 'What are you waiting for? Get on with it.` He was despatched with one single blow.

Lord Thomas Stanley was next to face the axe. He was the stepfather of Henry Tudor through his second marriage to the Lady Margaret Beaufort, Dowager Countess of Richmond. Tudor had based his shaky claim to the throne from his mother's descent from John of Gaunt, duke of Lancaster, third son of Edward 111, and his mistress, later his wife, Katherine Swynford. The children of this misalliance took the surname of Beaufort and were legitimised by Richard 11 with the proviso that they would have no legal claim to the throne.

Stanley was Margaret Beaufort's third husband and he was one of the wealthiest men in England, owning large tracts of land in both Lancashire and in Cheshire, One of his more bizarre titles being King of Mann. He had skilfully managed to steer a middle course throughout the wars between Lancaster and York and together with his younger brother William, had until now, ensured that at least one of them was always on the winning side in any conflict. Until the Battle of Bosworth, Thomas Stanley appeared to be Richard's man. He had borne the great Mace at his coronation while his wife Margaret, carried the Queen's train. Stanley also held the post of Steward of the Royal Household and even more importantly, Constable of England which included that of Constable of the Tower of London.

When Henry Tudor and his army landed in Wales and began their march towards the Midlands. Richard summoned Stanley, who at the time was visiting his lands in Lancashire, to rendezvous with him immediately together with his army of over two thousand men. Richard suspected that Stanley had been in touch with his stepson, probably at the behest of his wife, and his suspicions were confirmed when Stanley sent word to the King saying that regretfully, he could not march to join him as he was confined to his bed with the dreaded Sweating Sickness. However, Stanley and his men *did* arrive and on 22 August took up their position between the Royal Army and the Lancastrian rebels while his brother, together with his men, lined up opposite him. Stanley knelt, crossed himself and with a quick jerk of his hand, flicked his long beard forward as he placed his neck on the block. He too was despatched with one clean blow.

Sir William Stanley was next to meet the Executioner. Standing defiantly beside the block, he refused to kneel and was forced down by two burly assistants. As he knelt, one of his knees slipped on the accumulated blood oozing around the scaffold causing him to fall forward and gash his chin badly on the block. The last thing he saw before the headsman swung his axe was his brother's headless corpse being dragged away. During his career as a soldier, William Stanley had fought on the Yorkist side at the battles of both Blore Heath in 1459 and at Tewkesbury in 1471 where he had distinguished himself by capturing the Lancastrian Queen Margaret of Anjou following that momentous battle and was made a Knight Banneret by a grateful King Edward IV. In 1483 he was granted the Post of Chief Justice of North Wales for his loyal service by Richard so his desertion to the Lancastrian side at Bosworth shocked and hurt Richard deeply.

The executions over, Richard turned to his friends.

'Now that justice has been done, make all haste for preparations for our departure. We leave for London at first light tomorrow. Not you, Thomas' he said, laying a restraining hand on the earl of Surrey's arm as he prepared to leave the room. 'You must accompany your Lord father's body to his final resting place. Will it be in Norfolk?'

'Aye, Sire, in the Howard vault at Thetford Priory'

'I owe a debt of gratitude to both you and to your father, Thomas. I will never forget the loyalty of the dukes of Norfolk. When your affairs are settled, come to me, I will have need of you.'

The new duke of Norfolk bowed gravely and left the room.

# 2

Richard's heart sank as he and his cavalcade approached London. Memories came flooding back of the past traumatic two years since he became King, especially the shocking news in 1484 of the death his ten year old son and only heir, Edward, the frail Prince of Wales, at Middleham, Richard's stronghold in Wensleydale, Yorkshire from where he had ruled as Lord of the North during the reign of his brother, Edward IV. He would never forget the utter devastation the news of their son's death brought to himself and to his wife, Anne, made worse because they were not at home but staying at Nottingham Castle at the time.

Anne, the youngest of the two daughters of the late earl of Warwick, known as the 'Kingmaker' had always been delicate in health and the death of her only child accelerated the progress of her underlying lung disease resulting in her death at the far too young age of twenty eight, five months earlier on 16 March in Westminster Palace. The same disease had also contributed to the death following childbirth, of Anne's elder sister, Isabel, who was the wife of the late George, duke of Clarence, elder brother of Richard who was attainted of treason and executed in the Tower on the orders of his brother, Edward IV. The same lung disease was probably responsible for little Edward's untimely death also.

Despite the enthusiastic welcome from its citizens as he rode through the gates and into his capitol city, acknowledging the cheers with his quiet smile, Richard was acutely aware of the stench from the unwashed crowds of people and from the filth that littered the gutters made worse by the hot summer weather. The noise was deafening from the sound of church bells, trumpets and the beating of drums, not to mention the neighing of horses and the barking of dogs until the sounds were drowned out by the bells of St Paul's mighty Cathedral. The procession halted before the West Door where

Richard dismounted and approached the Bishop of London, the Dean and Chapter who waited to greet their King. Richard's nostrils was assoiled by the welcome sweet scent of incense as he knelt for the Bishop's blessing then to the sound of the organ thundering out a triumphant Te Deum, he arose and entered the Cathedral for the service of Thanksgiving for the victory at Bosworth.

As he progressed up the nave towards the High Alter, Richard glanced sideways and caught a glimpse of the tomb of John of Gaunt, duke of Lancaster, third surviving son of king Edward 111 who had died in 1399 and murmured to himself.

'Ah! Duke John, if only you knew what havoc your descendants have caused in poor England'


When the service ended the procession reformed and Richard mounted White Surrey once again and led the way down Ludgate Hill and on to the Strand, halting at Temple Bar where the Lord Mayor of London and members of the various City Trade Guilds waited to bid farewell to their King. Now free of the close confines of the city, the procession gathered speed as they rode towards the Royal Palace at Westminster. On their left hand side they passed several large town houses belonging to the nobility complete with large gardens running down to the banks of the Thames each with their own private landing stage. They next passed the impressive ruins of the Savoy Palace, former home of John of Gaunt that was destroyed during the Peasants Revolt against the hated Poll Tax back in 1381. The next landmark was the Charing Cross built by the grieving King Edward I to mark the final overnight resting place of his beloved Queen, Eleanor of Castile, prior to her burial in Westminster Abbey. Reaching the end of the Strand, the cavalcade passed by the Royal Mews, not the home of the royal stables but the home of the Falcons, Merlins, etc, used in the royal hawking parties who screeched and flapped their wings on their perches at the noise of the passing horses clattering hooves and the beating of the drums. Turning left, Richard finally entered the precincts of the Royal Palace of Westminster which straddled the banks of the Thames all the way down to Westminster Abbey.

On entering the royal apartments he was pleasantly surprised to be greeted by his Mother, Cecily, the Dowager duchess of York.

'My lady mother' His face breaking into a wide smile.' I didn't expect to find you here.' He kissed her hand and both cheeks.

'I had to be here to greet you today of all days. God bless you my son, I am so proud of you'

The Duchess smiled at her youngest and only surviving son. Still standing upright with only a few lines around her eyes that belied her seventy years, Cecily Neville still retained traces of the beauty that in her youth had earned her the epithet 'The Rose of Raby' after her family home in Co Durham and the less flattering 'Proud Cis' . She may have taken minor religious orders in her later years but Cicely's black and white habit was made from sumptuous white satin and black velvet adorned with a large gold crucifix hanging from a heavy golden chain studded with huge rubies around her neck.

Just then there was a commotion from the adjoining chamber followed by the door bursting open as a large grey Wolfhound bounded into the room and with a joyful bark, threw itself upon Richard, its paws on his shoulders causing him to stagger backwards from its frenzied greeting as the great dog licked his face, his furiously wagging tail knocking two wine goblets off a nearby table and sending them clattering to the floor. 'Down, Rex, down, Boy. That is quite enough' laughed Richard patting his four legged friend and managing to disentangle the front paws from his shoulders

'Oh, Sire, I'm reet sorry bout this but the mad 'ound heard yer voice an' broke loose afore I could stop 'im' Struggling to catch his breath, Tom Murgatroyd limped up to Richard who was leaning over Rex and rubbing his belly as he lay on his back with his paws in the air and his tongue lolling out of the side of his mouth as he writhed on the floor in ecstasy. 'No harm done, Tom', Richard replied as he carefully straightened up.

'That dog needs disciplining' Cecily remarked, fastidiously sweeping her skirts aside and taking a seat well out of the way of the boisterous hound. 'He is young and will learn' answered Richard straightening up and gingerly rubbing his back.

Rex had been Anne's final gift to him last Christmas. She knew that she was dying and that this Christmas would be her last as she

11

handed her husband the basket containing the wriggling puppy saying

'When I am gone this hound pup will be your faithful friend and he will love you almost as much as I do. I have named him Rex because he will be the King's Dog'

Richard sadly recalled Anne's loving smile before she was overtaken by a choking bout of coughing. From that day on Rex hardly ever left his master's side as he rapidly grew from a pup into the large hound who now flopped down beside him.

The following day Cecily left to return to her home at Berkhamsted Castle and to her largely contemplative lifestyle as Richard prepared to leave for the Tower and his first council meeting since his victory at Bosworth. Overnight the weather had changed from the previous hot, sun filled summer days to an overcast grey sky and a chilly wind that blew off the river that threatened rain. Attired in a rich black and purple doublet and matching hose enlightened by his customary gold chain linked with white Yorkist roses across his shoulders, and his favourite black velvet hat complete with its silver badge of the White Boar, Richard made an imposing figure as he began to draw on his leather gauntlets when Tom appeared carrying a heavy grey woollen cloak.

'I think your grace might need this today seein' as it will be cold on yon river' Jerking his thumb in the direction of the Thames. He reached up and placed the cloak over the King's shoulder.

'At least the cold wind should help to blow away the worse of the stench from there' Richard replied tying the cloak about his throat. ' I, Sire, it is a reet stink hole at the best of times' Tom nodded. 'But then I reckon the whole of London is one big bloody cesspit'

'So do I, Tom, so do I'

It was raining hard by the time that the royal barge arrived at the Tower and Richard was glad of the cloak as he stepped ashore to be greeted by Sir Robert Brackenbury, the Constable of the Tower who had also fought beside his king at Bosworth.

'Is everything in readiness, Brackenbury?' He asked.

'Aye, Sire' Brackenbury replied.

'Good, then let us get out of this foul weather' Shrugged Richard and hurried towards the Council chamber in the White Tower followed by his private secretary, John Kendal who struggled to keep up with him after being slightly wounded in the knee at Bosworth, and by Rex who bounded joyously ahead shaking himself dry.

'His grace the king,' announced a Squire. The members of the council all scrambled to their feet with a scraping of chairs as Richard entered the lofty chamber and took his seat on the throne like chair at the head of the long table.

'My lords, gentlemen, pray be seated. We have much business to attend to this day'

'Before we commence with the business in hand, may I, your grace, on behalf of all your loyal council members, congratulate your Grace on your great victory?'

The speaker was the aged archbishop of Canterbury and his remarks were followed by murmurs of agreement from around the table .' I thank you, gentlemen. Now to business' Richard answered gravely.

As the meeting progressed Richard knew that sooner rather than later the subject of his re-marriage would arise now that the country was stable again and free from threat of a Lancastrian invasion. He sighed inwardly but accepted that his need for an heir was paramount, even the thought of taking a new wife was repugnant to him so soon after the death of his beloved Anne.

Before that, however, the fate of the main conspirators who had plotted the Tudor invasion was discussed.

'John Morton, the traitorous bishop of Ely who had plotted with both the late duke of Buckingham and with the Lady Margaret Beaufort will be suitably punished,' Richard declared grimly.

'But, Sire,' interrupted Robert Stillington, the aged bishop of Bath and Wells, 'you cannot put a churchman to death, even if he is a traitor. You will risk your immortal soul.'

'I said he would be punished, my lord Bishop. I never mentioned executing him,' Richard interrupted. 'As we speak he is under armed guard from Ely to Barnard Castle up in Co Durham where he will be honourably, but closely confined so that he will no longer be in a position to plot any more mischief. As for the Lady Margaret Beaufort, Tudor's mother and Thomas Stanley's widow. I have dispatched Sir Ralph de Assheton and a troop of his men to her home at Collyweston and to bring her here to the Tower under lock and key until I decide what to do with her.'

'What of that bitch, the Woodville woman, the so-called former Queen?' Asked Francis Lovell with a harsh laugh, 'Will she be for the axe because by all that's holy she deserves it'

'No, Frank,' replied Richard. 'You know that I do not execute women. I have decided that she will live out her life across the river from here in Bermondsey Abbey. Her children may visit her if they wish to.'

'You are too lenient, Sire' William Catesby intervened speaking for the first time and shaking his head. 'The Woodvilles would not have hesitated to kill you to keep the power in their grasping hands'

'I am well aware of that, Will' Richard nodded in agreement. 'But I am thinking of her and my late brother's innocent children. They have suffered enough and Elizabeth Woodville is now powerless.'

The room fell silent and as Richard glanced around the table, he knew why most of the councillors would not meet his gaze but looked away or began to shuffle papers while some coughed awkwardly. He sighed inwardly. The councillors wanted to ask but none of them dared broach the subject, the fate of Richard's young nephews, Edward, briefly the king and Richard, the duke of York until Bishop Stillington's shock revelation that the marriage of their parents, King Edward IV and Elizabeth Woodville was bigamous because at the time of the ceremony, conducted in secret, Edward was already wed to lady Eleanor Butler, daughter of the earl of Shrewsbury in an earlier also secret ceremony, and therefore the boys and their sisters were bastards with no legal claim to the throne. At the time when this shock news broke, the boys were lodged in the royal apartments in the Tower as was customary before a King's coronation. They were there when Richard saw them for the last time, the day before he and Queen Anne left to go on progress following their coronation. When he eventually returned to London, the boys had disappeared and were never seen again and to his horror, Richard had no idea of what fate had befallen them.

# 3

'My lords, let us move on. What is next on the agenda?' he asked sharply.

'Ahem,' clearing his throat, the Speaker of the House of Commons, looking quite uncomfortable, rose to his feet. 'It is the question of your grace's future marriage and the need of an heir to your grace's throne.' The Speaker looked about him at the other council members who nodded in support.

'We, that is, the Council, believe the matter to be of some urgency.'

Richard grimaced, knowing that the subject he dreaded discussing was now out in the open and would have to be faced.

'As you know, my lords, I have named my nephew, John, the earl of Lincoln who is the eldest son of my sister Elizabeth, the duchess of Suffolk, as my heir. But I am well aware that I need an heir of *my* body to eventually, god willing, succeed me in the fullness of time. I have therefore opened negotiations with King John II of Portugal for the hand of his sister, the Princess Joanna.'

This news seemed to satisfy the men around the table who murmured their approbation.

'As you gentlemen will probably have realised, the match will be highly suitable as the princess is the great granddaughter of John of Gaunt, duke of Lancaster through his daughter, Philippa, and is undoubtedly a legitimate descendant of the house of Lancaster.'

Richard paused and smiled sardonically. 'Unlike the bastard Beaufort line.'

'Indeed, your grace,' answered the Speaker 'Your proposed match sounds eminently suitable.' As the rest of the council members nodded in agreement.

'May we ask your grace if your nephew and your nieces will now be returning to London now that it is safe for them to do so?' the archbishop of Canterbury ventured to enquire.

'Yes, I have put arrangements into place to bring them back from our castles at both Pontefract and from Sheriff Hutton now that the danger of invasion is past.'

'Hell's bell's!' interrupted Robert Percy. 'What or who is making that god awful racket?' he cried, leaping to his feet and opening the chamber door, closely followed by Rex who had been dozing quietly at Richard's feet beneath the table, but who was now barking wildly as his paws clattered noisily down the stone stairs and out onto Tower Green followed by the King and all the councillors.

The cause of all the noise was a woman screaming and yelling like a demented banshee as she struggled to free herself from two men at arms who were forcibly restraining her, despite her kicks to their shins.

'Let me go you miserable sons of Satan. How dare you treat me thus!'

'Restrain yourself, Madam, your actions are demeaning and unworthy of yourself.'

Richard immediately recognised Sir Ralph de Assheton's unmistakable Lancashire accent as he emerged from the White Tower and walked across the Green towards the pandemonium which by now had attracted a large crowd of curious onlookers who respectively stood aside to allow their King and his followers to move forward to the centre of the commotion where to his dismay, he came face to face with his arch enemy, the Lady Margaret Beaufort, dowager countess of Richmond and The mother of Henry Tudor.

The murmuring crowd fell silent as Richard and Lady Margaret eyed each other. the only sound was the sound of the steadily falling rain and the harsh cries of the Tower Ravens on their perches. Even Rex had stopped barking, restrained by Francis Lovell who gripped the hound's collar. Slowly, Margaret Beaufort raised her head then suddenly attempted to leap upon Richard but was quickly pulled back and held by Ralph de Assheton in a vice like grip, screaming,

'You murdering Yorkist bastard, you killed my son, Henry, my beautiful son. I hope you burn in Hell.'

16

Flinging back her head, she aimed a mouthful of spittle which missed his face but ran down his doublet in an obscene mess as he stepped back. 'I am glad that your son died, Gloucester!' she screamed. 'And glad that I and stupid, deluded, Buckingham killed your bastard nephews while you and your mealy mouthed wife were away on your so called progress.'

Leaping forward, his eyes blazing, Richard grasped her shoulders, and shook her. 'You *and* Buckingham were responsible for the murder of those two innocent children?' he shouted.

'Aye,' she laughed. 'Buckingham and I watched whilst they were suffocated. It did not take long.'

The shocked onlookers exchanged looks of amazement and started to murmur amongst themselves. Stepping back from her, Richard asked quietly, 'Where are they now? Where did you have them buried?'

'Ah, Gloucester, that's for me to know and for you to guess. Look around you, where will you start? The Tower is such a large place,' Margaret Beaufort gloated, her eyes wild and her greying hair blowing wildly about her head from which her head dress had become dislodged during her struggles with her captors.

'Take her away,' ordered Richard quietly, suddenly feeling tired and drained of energy.

Francis Lovell, forgetting court etiquette in his excitement, rushed to Richard's side and grasped his arm.

'You know what this means, Dickon, don't you?' he said breathlessly. 'It only means that after today, in front of all these witnesses, no one will ever be able to accuse you of murdering your nephews ever again.'

'Aye, Frank,' he replied sombrely, 'I realise that and confess that it is a load off my mind, but the fact remains that my nephews are definitely dead and that I failed to keep them safe. I must learn to live with that guilt. Come, let us get out of this place and return to Westminster.'

As he began to walk down towards the Tower's riverside gate with a now subdued Rex trotting quietly beside him. The assembled crowd began to cheer amid cries of 'God save your grace' that followed him until he boarded his barge with a last glance at the brooding fortress before he gave the order to the waiting boatmen to begin rowing back up the Thames to Westminster Palace.

# 4

It was mid-October and the hot summer had moved on to a glorious autumn with all the trees ablaze with colour. A final show of nature's splendour before the colourful leaves began to fall, heralding the onset of winter.

The court was at Windsor, the one place within a day's ride of London where Richard could relax and unwind and enjoy hunting in Windsor's great park away from the capitol's stifling atmosphere.

Above the din of the many horses clattering into the castle courtyard at the end of a successful days hunt, the king, laughing genially at one of Francis Lovell's more outrageous quips, led the way with his companions close behind him. Servants were waiting for the hunting party to dismount before leading the tired horses to a welcoming drink of water, food, and a cooling rub down before settling into their stables. The hunting hounds flopped down, panting with their tongues hanging out. Replete after eating part of the day's kill as their reward.

Once indoors, Richard drew off his leather gauntlets and tossed them to a waiting squire before gulping down a tankard of cool ale handed to him by another retainer.

'Ah! That's better' he beamed handing the tankard back to another kneeling retainer.

'I have your grace's bath and clean clothes ready' spoke up Tom Murgatroyd, hovering in the background, just as the Household Steward entered the chamber and bowing deeply to the king, announced

'Sire, Sir Edward Brampton arrived from Portugal about two hours ago and begs for an audience at your grace's convenience ` 'The bath will have to wait, Tom, I must attend to this matter first,' called Richard, and turning to the Steward, went on, ' I will see Sir Edward now. Pray bid him enter.'

Sir Edward Brampton had served the House of York as a loyal wartime commander for many years. Originally a Jew from Portugal, he had converted to Christianity taking the name of Edward from King Edward IV who had stood as his godfather at his baptism.

His loyalty to his new king and country was legendary. A large man whose swarthy complexion, dark greying hair and eyes proclaimed his southern European roots.

Because of his Portuguese background and his trustworthiness, Richard judged him to be his ideal Ambassador to present his proposal of marriage to the Princess Joanna to her brother, King John, and to also propose a match between his niece, the former Princess Elizabeth of York, now known as the Lady Elizabeth, to the King's cousin, Manuel, the Duke of Breja.

'Sir Edward Brampton, your grace.' Advancing towards the King, Brampton dropped to his knees before Richard who, noticing Brampton's grave demeanour, ordered all but his closest friends to leave the chamber and to close the door behind them.

'What news from Portugal do you bring me, Edward?' Richard gestured to him to rise. 'From your expression I doubt it is good.'

'Aye, the news is not good, your grace.' Brampton nervously twisted his hat in his hands and coughed nervously before continuing.

'King John bade me give your grace his apologies but said that the proposed marriage cannot take place because the Princess Joanna has taken minor holy orders, including a vow of chastity prior to her taking the veil.'

Richard supressed a sigh of relief that the dreaded but necessary marriage would not now take place.

'And what of the marriage of the Lady Elizabeth and the duke of Breja?' he asked.

Brampton looked even more uncomfortable. 'I don't know how to say this, Sire,' he mumbled.

'Spit it out man,' he barked impatiently.

'The king won't consent to that marriage because in his own words, Sire, not mine, he said that it would not be fitting for Duke Manuel to marry a bastard, even if she is the daughter of a king.'

Sir Edward glanced warily at the King and was amazed to see what momentarily looked like relief cross Richard's face before his features regained their customary impassive expression

'Thank you, Sir Edward, for your diligence in reporting the results of your assignment to me so honestly. It cannot have been an easy task for you.'

Richard patted Brampton's shoulder bidding him to, 'Sit down and take your ease with a goblet of wine.'

'I thank your grace.' Visibly relieved, Brampton sat down, gratefully accepting his drink in one hand from Ralph de Assheton and mopping his perspiring face with his other.

'Get this this down you,' joked Ralph. 'I know you think that you are an Englishman now, but you still prefer foreign wine to good honest English ale.'

'Oh leave him be, Ralph,' laughed Rob Percy, 'And let the man enjoy his wine in peace.'

'How did you find Portugal, Sir Edward?' Richard Ratcliffe asked quizzically, when the laughter had died down.

'Changed,' Brampton replied thoughtfully. 'It was a strange feeling being back there again after so many years away. I felt like a stranger in what was once my homeland.' He shrugged his shoulders and with a grin towards Ralph de Assheton continued, 'Despite the hot weather and the good local wine.'

After a few moments, the King questioned Brampton again.

'What else, if anything, did King John have to say?'

Placing his now empty goblet onto a table, Brampton answered, 'Sire, his grace spoke of his regret that a marriage alliance between our two nations could not take place at this moment in time but expressed the hope that both Portugal and England remained good friends and allies.'

'Thank you, Sir Edward,' nodded Richard.

Brampton spoke again, 'After I left the King's presence, I was approached by a Page who asked me to accompany him to the Princess Joanna's apartment as she wished to speak to me in private. Somewhat surprised by this request, I followed the Page to the chamber where, attended by two ladies and her confessor, she greeted me most courteously. She asked me to inform your grace that she was deeply honoured by your proposal and that if she hadn't been called by God to serve him, it would have been her great pleasure to become your queen.'

Brampton paused and put his hand into the purse that hung from his belt and withdrew a small black leather box. Kneeling, he presented it to a stunned Richard who turned it over in his hand.

Brampton resumed. 'Her Highness bade me give this token of her esteem to your grace and to tell you that you that you would always be in her prayers.'

His curiosity aroused, Richard opened the box to find it sumptuously lined with black velvet and containing a beautiful ivory and golden rosary with the eyes on the figure of Christ made from minute sapphires. Richard was momentarily stuck for words as he carefully lifted his gift from the box and bending his head, placed it around his neck before speaking to Brampton again.

'Sir Edward, pray convey my sincere thanks to the princess for this beautiful, unexpected gift which I shall treasure, and also for her kind words.'

'I will send your message by swift courier immediately, your grace,' bowed Brampton.

'What does the princess look like?' asked Francis Lovell. 'Is she beautiful?'

'The princess is small, with a gentle serene face framed by her nun's wimple, and very dignified,' answered Brampton.

'It seems that England has lost one who would have been an ideal queen,' said Richard Ratcliffe regretfully to murmurs of agreement.

'I suppose that the search must go on,' mused Richard, fingering the rosary thoughtfully.

'It shouldn't prove too difficult a search,' interrupted William Catesby, tapping his lower lip with his index finger. 'After all, your grace is now the most eligible prince in Europe.'

'Aye,' chortled Rob Percy, 'you can have your pick. What does your grace prefer: blonde, brunette or how about a fiery redhead? Short, tall, thin or fat?'

This remark was greeted by loud laughter, even producing a grin from Richard.

'Enough, gentlemen,' He held up his hands and the laughter died down. 'Let us now away and make ourselves ready for dinner. Will, Francis, attend on me.' The men arose and bowed as Richard, followed by William Catesby and by Francis Lovell left the room.

# 5

Tom Murgatroyd stepped forward and bowed as the king and his two friends entered his private chamber to be greeted by a wildly excited Rex who had been dozing quietly with his head between his paws by the fire until he heard his master's voice approaching.

'I will take my bath now, Tom' said Richard, stroking the hound.

'I have kept the water hot so all is ready, your grace.'

Answered Tom as he began to help the King to disrobe with a sideways glance at Lovell and at Catesby.

'I have a matter of some importance to discuss with these gentlemen, Tom. I can rely on your discretion on anything you just happen to overhear?'

'Of course, your grace,' grinned Tom. 'I knows 'ow to keep me gob shut.'

Once Richard was settled into his bath with Tom sponging his back and his two friends sitting on the other side of the fireplace, he brought up the subject of his marriage again.

'Have you any suggestions as to where I can widen my search for a bride, my friends?'

'It is a pity that Queen Isabella of Castile is married. But saying that, she has several daughters' offered Catesby.

'Oh no, Will,' Richard said frowning.

'Isabella is around my age so her daughters are far too young to be considered. I need a lady of an age who can provide me with an heir now. I cannot afford to wait until the Spanish princesses are old enough to bear children'

'How about a French match then?' Continued Catesby.

'I believe that the Duc de Orleons has an eligible daughter'

'God's breath, spare us another French woman, Will'

Francis Lovell burst out.

'England does not want another Margaret of Anjou'

'You are quite right there, Frank' Agreed Richard.

They all fell silent as they remembered the Queen, wife of the Lancastrian King, Henry V1 and the havoc she had caused during the recent 'cousins 'war'

'Well ' Said Catesby wrinkling his brow.

'That leaves us with contenders from the Holy Roman Empire in Germany and Austria, the Italian states, or the Scandinavian countries.'

'Hmm...,' mused Richard, glancing at Lovell whose facial expression was unusually thoughtful.

'You have gone very quiet, Frank.'

'I have been thinking, Dickon,' he replied, addressing the King informally as they were in private.

'Have you ever considered a match nearer home?'

'You mean our King should marry an Englishwoman?' Catesby butted in before Richard had time to reply.

'No, if you will allow me to finish,' Turning to Richard he continued. 'I meant have you considered an alliance with Scotland, Dickon? It could bring many advantages, maybe even a lasting peace to our northern border.'

'No, that thought never occurred to me.'

Richard rose from the steaming bath and Tom was waiting with a large warm towel which he quickly wrapped around the King's soaking wet body.

Richard was deep in thought as now warm and dry, Tom began assisting him to dress in a clean white linen shirt and a brown velvet doublet and matching hose. He spoke again.

'Your idea has given me plenty of food for thought, Frank. Do you know if there are any suitable Scottish ladies available?'

'Well, Dickon, the present king, James III, has three young sons but no daughters. Even if he had, they would be far too young for you. But, he has a sister, the Princess Mary, who is a widow with two young children, and she is about your age'

'My, Frank,' grinned Richard. 'You have been busy.'

'I have made it my business to know about these things,' he laughed.

23

'Come, let us all to dinner and give some more thought to Frank's suggestion,' called Richard, leading the way to the great hall and to the appetising aroma of roasting meats.

During the next few days when the court had returned to Westminster, Richard thought long and hard about the possibility of a marriage alliance with Scotland, and the more he thought about it, the more he warmed to the idea.

Before the question of a Scottish marriage had arisen, Richard had arranged for Sir William Catesby to travel to Edinburgh as his ambassador to consult with King James on his behalf on the ongoing lawlessness on the English/Scottish border, perpetrated by certain 'riding' Families known as ' the Reivers' led on the Scottish side by the Kerr's, Armstrong's, and the Scott's and on the English side by the Charlton's, Hall's and Fenwick's amongst many others. They continuously raided over the border, 'lifting 'Cattle and burning and looting, and when they were not raiding across the border, they carried on lifelong feuds with each other. A law unto themselves, they acknowledged neither king as their overlord.

Two days later, Richard had reached a decision and summoned Catesby and Lovell to his presence. Signalling them to be seated, he came straight to the point.

'After much deliberation, I have decided that the idea of a Scottish match is a good one,' he began. 'But it depends on one or two things that I need to be sure about. First, that King James is agreeable to the match, and secondly,' he paused and grinning at Lovell said, 'and this is where you come in, Frank.'

'Me?'

Richard cut him off. 'Yes, you, Frank. I want you to accompany Will to Scotland and discreetly, mind you, look the princess over and let me know what you think of her. I want someone whom I can Trust to give me an honest opinion as to her manner and appearance, oh, and try to sound her out on how she may feel about a new marriage'

'Phew!! You are asking an awful lot of me, Dickon.' Lovell let out a long breath.

'Are you sure that I am the right person for such an important assignment?'

'I cannot think of anyone else that I would trust with this task,' said Richard seriously.

'Now my friends, You depart in three days time so you will have many preparations to make for your journey.'

He paused before resuming,

'You are both well aware that I have instituted a very reliable courier service with trusty riders placed at strategic points between here and Scotland. Make full use of them when you have news for me. Hopefully, I should receive any message from you in about a week's time.'

# 6

The day of departure had arrived and surrounded by all their friends, Including Catesby's tearful wife, Margaret, Richard stood in the courtyard to bid farewell to Lovell and to Catesby as they mounted their horses and accompanied by their retainers, baggage cart and a group of twenty armed men at arms, prepared to set off on their long journey. He told them to, 'Take care and try to get back before Christmas or you will be cut off by the winter snows'

After many overnight stops en route at places like Northampton, Leicester, Nottingham, Pontefract and York. They finally crossed the border into Scotland after spending the previous night at Berwick – Upon – Tweed. Travelling at a steady pace, they entered Edinburgh fourteen days after leaving London. The sky was overcast and a chill wind gave the promise of rain as at last the weary travellers rode up the Lawn Market to their lodgings at the foot of Castle Hill in the shadow of Edinburgh's great brooding castle which they noticed was flying the Royal Standard of Scotland from its highest tower indicating that the King of Scots was in residence. The sound of their clattering Horses hooves into the courtyard of the large hostelry brought the Landlord running out to greet them as he recognised them as guests of importance.

'Welcome, my lords,' he cried, bowing profusely, 'Welcome.'

He signalled to the waiting grooms to take care of the horses then led the way indoors.

After ensuing that their escorts were settled in with food and comfortable beds for the night. Lovell and Catesby sat at their ease before a roaring fire with a goblet of wine following an excellent meal.

'Well, Frank, I bet you got a better welcome this time than when you last came to this town with Gloucester as Richard was then, back in 1482?'

Aye' that's true '

Lovell nodded in agreement, his memory returning to the invasion of Scotland planned by Richard's brother, Edward IV. Who not well enough in health to lead his army, put Richard in command in his stead. Richard successfully re-took the vital border town of Berwick - Upon - Tweed from the Scots and marched the army virtually unopposed into Scotland. The Scots surrendered to Richard's superior forces and then he led his army into Edinburgh where he enforced his strict rule of no molesting or looting of the local populace before he eventually returned to England in triumph.

'Did you actually get to see King James?' Catesby asked.

'Yes. He had been imprisoned in the castle during an earlier insurrection and Dickon freed him'

'How did he strike you, Frank?'

'In a word, hapless, I was not impressed.' Lovell shook his head. 'He struck me as indecisive, one who cannot make up his mind or stick to a decision.' He laughed. 'When he gets around to making on'

'Then our task is not going to be an easy one,' sighed Catesby, stifling a yawn. 'I don't know about you, Frank, but I am dog tired and am now away to my bed.'

'Me also,' agreed Lovell, downing the last of his wine. 'We have a busy day ahead of us tomorrow.'


The following day dawned with clear skies and with the sun casting a warm autumn glow over the rooftops and the wynds of the old city as Catesby and Lovell, attired in full court dress, Lovell in deep blue and white velvet doublet and matching cloak, hat and hose that enhanced his blond colouring, together with a heavy gold chain about his shoulders with his device of the dog dangling from the centre.

Catesby was looking his best in the bold Gold colours that suited his dark hair and complexion complete with a Silver and emerald studded chain.

Accompanied by their men at arms, they rode across the esplanade to the castle entrance to present their credentials to the king. Word had earlier been sent ahead to request an audience with the king which had been granted.

They were met and greeted by the castle Steward and escorted through various rooms and corridors until they arrived outside the Audience chamber guarded by two stalwart guardsmen armed with Halberds who sprang forward to open the stout wooden doors as the Steward, about to announce the visitors, was stopped in his tracks by the sound of music coming from inside the chamber where a young woman was singing a beautiful lilting melody while accompanying herself on a lute. The King sitting in his chair of state on a raised dais, raised a warning finger for silence then waved his other hand to summon his visitors forward as the song came to an end and the final chords of the lute faded away.

'Viscount Lovell and Sir William Catesby, may it please your grace,' intoned the Steward as Lovell and Catesby walked towards the dais then knelt as the King rose to his feet and extended his hand for them to kiss.

'You are both very welcome, my lords, please arise'

Turning, he gestured to the lady with the lute who rose gracefully from her seat and stepped forward.

'Gentlemen, this lady with the beautiful voice is my dear sister, The Princess Mary, Lady Hamilton.'

# 7

Catesby and Lovell caught each other's eye at the surprise introduction but both men quickly recovered their composure, bowed and kissed the Princess's hand.

'I am very happy to meet you, my lords and to add my welcome to Scotland'

Princess Mary spoke in a low but clear voice enhanced by her musical Scottish accent.

'Your Highness is most kind'

Replied Catesby while Lovell gazed at her, momentarily lost for words. He saw a young woman, slightly built of average height with a heart shaped face crowned by a glimpse of dark auburn hair just visible beneath her widow's headdress with its flowing white veil, a sumptuous gown of grey and white velvet and silk completed her appearance.

But what struck Lovell the most were her eyes, a distinctive shade of deep blue, almost violet in their intensity. Recovering himself, Lovell murmured,

'Your servant, your Highness'

'I will leave you to your business now, gentlemen, brother' dropping a curtsey to the king, the princess Mary turned and left the chamber as the halberdiers sprang forward to open the doors for her.

Neither Catesby or Lovell could believe their good fortune in meeting the princess so unexpectedly on their first full day in Edinburgh and found it hard to concentrate on their talks with the King.

Early the following morning as they were enjoying their breakfast, they were surprised to receive a summons from the king's wife, Queen Margaret, to attend her at eleven of the clock in her private chamber in the castle. Their curiosity thoroughly aroused, they arrived on time and were immediately escorted into the Queen's presence.

The daughter of King Christian I, of Denmark, Norway and Sweden, the three realms being united at that period of time.

She sat at her tapestry frame, deftly applying her needle to the elaborate pattern before her. She was surrounded by her attendant ladies in front of a blazing fire, a necessity as the days were now distinctly chillier. Also in attendance, sitting on her sister- in – law's right was the Princess Mary who glanced up and smiled as the visitors entered

'I thank you, my lords, for attending me at such short notice'

Queen Margaret spoke good English but with a strong Scandinavian accent. Dismissing all her ladies, with the exception of the Princess Mary, with a wave of her bejewelled hand, she graciously inclined her head towards her guests as they knelt before her. Bidding them to rise and be seated.

Catesby and Lovell glanced quickly at the Queen and noted that she was an intelligent rather than a beautiful looking young woman in her late twenties whose sharp eyes had already assessed both men.

She wasted no time in small talk, immediately coming to the point of the summons.

'I hope that the peace talks with his grace the King yesterday went well. But, vital as those discussions were, I believe they were not the only reason for your mission to Scotland at this time.'

Queen Margaret smiled as both Catesby and Lovell squirmed uncomfortably in their seats. They had certainly not expected this turn of events.

Catesby coughed awkwardly before replying, 'I am not sure of your grace's meaning.'

'Oh come now, Sir William.' With a nod in Lovell's direction, the Queen continued, 'My Lord Lovell, I assume that you are here to sound out the possibility of a royal marriage. Am I correct in my assumption?'

'King Richard is a widower, without an heir,' blustered Lovell, going red in the face, but a look of warning from Catesby silenced him.

'We are well aware of King Richard's marital situation,' smiled the Queen, amused by the Englishmen's reaction to her forthright speech.

'So I ask you again, my lords, are you here to negotiate a marriage between Scotland and England?'

During this exchange the Princess Mary had remained a silent witness who nevertheless, listened intently.

Francis Lovell, with a slight almost imperceptible nod from Catesby, decided that the straight talking Queen deserved a straight answer.

'Yes, your grace. My king believes that an alliance between our two nations would be beneficial to us both—'

Before he could elaborate he was interrupted by Princess Mary.

'My lord Lovell,' she spoke calmly but at the same time in a manner that demanded an answer. 'I presume that I am the prospective bride in question as there are no other suitable Scottish ladies available at this present time.'

'Yes, as your highness is the daughter and the sister of a king, you are of eminently suitable rank to become Queen of England,' Lovell replied, relieved that the matter was now out in the open.

'Did you bring up this subject during your talks with my brother yesterday?' Princess Mary asked.

'No, your highness. We merely discussed the problems on both sides of the border.'

'Ah,' said the Princess with a laugh. 'You wished to inspect me first, no doubt.'

'Come, sister,' the Queen spoke again. 'You are embarrassing these good gentlemen who, no doubt, will be sending a messenger to King Richard armed with a detailed description of your person.'

'Ah yes, but that works both ways. I must confess that I am curious about what kind of person King Richard is,' Princess Mary answered.

'King Richard is an honest, kindly man. Somewhat serious...,' began Catesby.

'But with a sense of humour,' Lovell quickly interjected. 'He is also a lover of music and of books and is also of course, a great warrior.'

'He sounds almost too good to be true,' mused the princess thoughtfully. 'But what does he look like?'

'He is about my height,' answered Catesby. 'Slightly built, with brown hair and blue-grey eyes.'

'I expect he is just as curious about me,' the princess answered.

'Yes indeed,' agreed Lovell, grinning.

'May we therefore inform his Grace that your highness is favourably inclined towards the marriage?'

'Yes, if my brother the king is agreeable. As you gentlemen will be aware, I am also the mother of two young children and I would wish to take them to England with me.'

The Queen interrupted, 'I am sure that there will be no problem with that arrangement.'

Catesby and Lovell exchanged amused glances, both now having got the measure of the no nonsense Queen.

'You gentlemen will doubtless have many matters to attend to,' said the Queen as she and the Princess rose to their feet. 'So we will not detain you any further today, but will inform you of the King's consent to this most appropriate match, when it pleases him too give it.'

'We thank your grace and your highness,' Catesby replied as both he and Lovell bowed deeply.

'And we in turn will report to yourselves and to his grace king James on any news that we expect to receive from King Richard.'

# 8

Meanwhile, back in London, Richard welcomed back to court the five daughters of his late brother, Edward IV and the orphaned son and daughter of his other brother George, duke of Clarence, executed for treason by Edward IV. He also welcomed his own illegitimate son, fifteen year old John of Pontefract. They had all been sent north to Richard's castle at Sheriff Hutton, near York for safety when the threat of an invasion from Henry Tudor became real.

Richard's face lit up in a smile as his young relatives entered the chamber, led by his eldest niece, nineteen year old Elizabeth, holding the hand of her youngest sister Bridget, who at the young age of six, was already a novice nun at Deptford Priory having been given to the order by her parents. Cecily sixteen, Anne eleven and Catherine seven, came next and all curtseyed deeply to their uncle.

They were followed by the Clarence children, twelve year old Margaret, trying her best to restrain her exuberant brother Edward, earl of Warwick, who leapt forward and ran to embrace Richard with a cry of.

'My lord uncle, I have so much to tell you. We have been to Sheriff Hutton. That is in Yorkshire you know'

'Yes, Ned, I do know that,' laughed Richard, gently disentangling himself from the excited boy.

'I am so sorry, my lord uncle for Ned's lack of manners.'

Margaret said, frantically trying to hold on to Edward.

'There is no need to apologise, Margaret, Ned cannot help it' Her uncle replied softly.

Edward was ten years old but only had the mental capacity of a five year old. Following the deaths of both their parents, Richard and Anne had taken the children to live with them and their own young son, also called Edward, at their home at Middleham castle in Wensleydale, so they were especially close to him.

Finally, he greeted his son John, raising him up as he knelt before him.

'No ceremony today, lad,' he said as he embraced him.

'I was so relieved and proud to hear of your victory, my lord father,' the young man murmured. 'And that you were safe and well.'

'Thank you, son,' Richard replied, deeply moved and marvelling once again how like him in appearance young John was growing.

He then moved into the centre of the chamber and announced with a smile, 'Go now and settle yourselves down in your chambers until we all meet again later for dinner.'

As the children turned to leave, Richard caught the eye of Elizabeth and signalled to her to approach him.

'A word if you please, Bess.'

'My lord uncle?' she asked with a puzzled frown.

'Yes, come with me.'

Richard led the way into his inner sanctum, a small comfortably furnished chamber where he conducted most of his daily business.

'Have I done something to displease you, my lord uncle?' Elizabeth asked nervously.

'Of course not, Bess,' Richard reassured her quietly. 'It is about your proposed marriage. I am very sorry to have to tell you that your marriage to the duke of Breja will not now take place.'

Elizabeth looked startled for a second and then to Richard's surprise, a huge grin lit up her face transforming her appearance completely from the anxious girl into a beautiful young woman.

'Oh, uncle Richard!' she cried. 'I am so glad that I do not have to go to Portugal. I would much rather stay here.'

'Really, you are pleased that duke Manuel has rejected you?'

'I suppose it is because I am no longer a princess, but if that means that I can stay here in England, then I don't care.' Elizabeth twirled round in a circle clapping her hands joyfully.

'Well,' mused Richard. 'I certainly didn't expect that reaction. It may be of interest to you to know that I will not be having a Portuguese Queen as the Princess Joanna has taken holy orders.'

'Oh please forgive me, my lord uncle,' Elizabeth cut short her merriment. 'I am so sorry that your proposed marriage will not now take place.'

'My thanks, Bess, but it is not the end of the world.' He smiled. 'Go and join your sisters now.'

'Thank you, uncle Richard, and thank you especially for getting rid of the Tudor. I couldn't bear the thought of marrying him and I also want you to know that I never thought for one second that you were capable of murdering my two brothers'

She briefly laid her hand on his arm, curtseyed deeply then turned and left the room.

The next day Richard received two important messages.

The first from Catesby and Lovell in Edinburgh via his efficient team of couriers.

He was relieved to learn that the Princess Mary had made such a good impression on them and that she was willing to become England's next queen, subject to King James' consent.

The second message brought bad news. Francis Lovell's wife, the former Anne Fitzhugh, was dead at the age of twenty nine. She had died three days earlier from a virulent fever at their home, Minster Lovell in Oxfordshire.

Although Lovell rarely mentioned his wife to him or to anyone else, Richard knew that his friend's marriage had never been a happy one. Married by arrangement at the age of twelve, they had nothing in common with each other and no children had been born to them. As the years passed they grew even more apart, hardly ever residing under the same roof, while Francis spent more and more time in attendance on Richard. With a sigh, Richard sat down at his desk and wrote a letter of condolence to Lovell that would be forwarded to Edinburgh in due course.

The king summoned his privy council to a meeting in the palace the following morning and just before noon Richard informed the assembled lords and commons that he had decided after much deliberation, to formally sue for the hand of the Princess Mary of Scotland. The Council members looked at each other in surprise at the unexpected news.

'As you are now aware, my lords, my proposed marriage to the Princess Joanna of Portugal cannot now take place and as my need for an heir is of paramount importance, an alliance with Scotland seems most appropriate at this time,' continued Richard.

Bishop Stillington rose from his seat and asked.

'Will your grace require a papal dispensation for this marriage to proceed?'

'I think not, my lord Bishop as we are not related in the forbidden degree,' Richard answered.

'What do we know about the lady?' The Speaker of The House of Commons was the next to comment.

'The princess is sister to King James, a widow and the mother of two young children,' remarked Richard. 'And is therefore an eminently suitable match.'

'And most importantly, the lady has proven that she is capable of bearing children,' commented Sir Ralph de Assheton with a wink that caused ripples of ribald laughter to resound around the room, including a grin from the king himself. When the laughter died down, Richard informed them that the message containing his formal offer of marriage would be forwarded to Scotland without delay.


Francis Lovell stared at the king's letter in disbelief. Anne, Dead? He read the missive again still unable to believe his eyes.

'What is it, Frank?' Catesby asked quietly on seeing his friend's stunned expression.

'It's Anne. She is dead. I have let her down again. I should have been with her.'

'You have nothing to reproach yourself with, Frank.'

Catesby laid a sympathetic hand on Lovell's shoulder before continuing.

'It wasn't your fault that she always kept you at a distance.'

'I know, Will. I wish that things had been different between us but it is too late now. I should at least have been present at her burial.'

'There is no way that you could have got back home to Minster Lovell in time for that from here in Edinburgh.'

'Aye. I suppose you are right, Will,' Lovell shrugged folding the letter and tucked it into his doublet.

'What has Richard to say?'

Catesby was carefully reading the king's missive. 'Richard has enclosed his formal request for the hand of the Princess to King James so we must ask for an audience without delay,' replied Catesby.

King James agreed to receive the two Englishmen the following afternoon in the castle Throne room accompanied by Queen Margaret seated beside him on her slightly lower throne. The King was a young man of thirty three but looked much older. Tall and thin with a large pointed nose that dominated his long face. seated on a stool on his right side sat his twelve year old eldest son and heir, James, Duke of Rothesay. The younger James, luckily for him, had not inherited his father's looks. He resembled his mother and already showed all the signs of the handsome young man he would become in the future.

Notable by her absence was the Princess Mary.

'Welcome, my lords.'

The king signalled them to come forward. ' I presume that you have news for us from king Richard?' He asked in his strong Scottish accent.

'Yes, your grace' Catesby answered. 'My King commands Viscount Lovell and myself to give you greetings and to ask for your royal consent to his marriage with your grace's sister, The Princess Mary'

'Ah' King James glanced sideways at his Queen who smiled back at him with a barely discernible nod.

'We have given this matter much thought, gentlemen, and we have decided that such an alliance would be beneficial to both our nations. Ye may inform King Richard that I will gladly welcome him as a brother'

'On behalf of our King, we thank your grace. We will send the word to London without delay so that all the necessary arrangements can be put in place before the onset of winter'

Lovell bowed deeply as he answered the king.

'Aye, the lassie needs to make haste to begin her journey south before the snows arrive'

Rising from his throne, James extended his hand to be kissed by the visitors then with a nod, he left the throne Room leaving his Queen to follow.

'Come, my lords, we will speak with the princess'

Queen Margaret led the way to the princess's chamber where they found her kneeling on the rush covered floor playing with her two children, six year old Robert and his four year old sister, Elizabeth, who were throwing a soft ball to a small white dog who yapped excitedly as he tried to catch it.

'You caught me unawares, my lords '

Hastily straightening her skirts as she rose to her feet, Mary turned to the children bidding them to be quiet while she spoke to her visitors.

'Judging from your smiles, you must have brought me good news' she continued.

'Yes, your highness.'

Both Catesby and Lovell replied simultaneously.

'His grace king Richard has offered you his hand in marriage,' said Catesby, ' o which your royal brother has gladly given his consent.'

At which point Queen Margaret interrupted stepping forward and kissed Mary on both cheeks.

'My congratulations, Sister, you will make a fine Queen of England'

Lovell next came forward and dropped on one knee before the princess offering her a package sealed with the arms of the king of England.

'I am commanded by my king to give this missive into your highness's hands alone.'

'I thank his grace,' she replied accepting the document and tucking it securely into her belt.

'And I will write him a reply forthwith,' she assured him.

Just then the ball rolled to a stop beside Lovell who was now standing upright again, so he reached down and picked it up and offered it to the little boy who had slithered to a halt before him closely followed by the small dog.

'Robert, I told you to stop playing with that wretched ball.' Princess Mary admonished her son who hung his head and shuffled his feet. 'Whatever will Lord Lovell think of you? Apologise immediately.'

'I am sorry, my lord and my Lady mother,' he muttered.

'No harm done, lad, ' said Lovell with a laugh as he bent down to stroke the small dog.

'I shudder to imagine what King Richard would think of such unruly behaviour,' the princess remarked.

'Oh, the king loves children and I am sure that he will adore these two young imps when he gets to know them,' Lovell reassured her.

'Never the less, I will ensure that their manners will improve,' the princess promised, trying not to smile as little Elizabeth reached for her mother's hand.

It was late in the afternoon before Princess Mary got a quiet moment when she could at last get the chance to read Richard's letter. She was greatly reassured by his message in which he said how happy he would be to welcome her to England and promised that he would treat her children like his own. She quickly penned a reply, thanking him for his kindness and for the honour he did to herself and to Scotland. She then sealed her letter and summoned a trusty servant to deliver it to Catesby and Lovell at their lodgings immediately.

A week later, Richard sitting at his desk in Westminster Palace, read Mary's reply for the second time. He let out a sigh realizing that there was no going back now and that he was committed to going through with this marriage even though he felt that he was betraying his beloved Anne. Hearing the sigh, Sir Richard Ratcliffe raised his head from the book he was reading in a corner of the room and quietly asked his old friend.

'Is all well, Dickon?' Using his boyhood name. 'You sound troubled.'

'This Scottish marriage, Dick. I know that I have to go through with it now, but I feel that I am betraying Anne.'

Ratcliffe closed his book and walked over to Richard.

'I understand that the lady in question is widowed too. Perhaps she feels the same way as you do, Dickon.'

'I never thought of that, Dick. Maybe we will have something in common. Thank you.'

Richard stood up and clicked his fingers to Rex who lay dozing with his head resting on his paws in front of the fire but on hearing his master, leapt to his feet and followed Richard from the room.

# 9

The Following three weeks were hives of frantic activity on both sides of the border as preparations for the royal marriage and for Princess Mary's journey south began. King James had commanded his entire court to escort the Princess and her two children as far as the border where they would say their farewells before the Princess entered England at Berwick - Upon –Tweed to be met and welcomed by representatives of the northern English nobility led by the earl of Northumberland. From there she would gradually move south with overnight halts at Bamburgh and at Dunstanburgh, Alnwick and Warkworth with a longer stop in the city of Durham before arriving in York where Richard decided he would meet her and that their marriage would take place in York Minster.

Due to the time of year and the possibility of an early onset of winter. He also informed the council and parliament that he would govern the country from his castle at Sheriff Hutton near York until the spring when the court would return to Westminster.

Richard, mounted on White Surrey, set off at a steady trot accompanied by his closest friends and government ministers and his body servant, Tom Murgatroyd, riding in one of the baggage carts along with Rex the dog, set off from Westminster Palace on the morning of a fine, but chilly 8 of November on the first stage of the almost two hundred mile journey to York. Following at a more leisurely pace were his nephew and nieces and their escorts.

The Scottish contingent had left Edinburgh two days earlier on the 6th on a grey, overcast day that threatened rain with a stiff wind that blew inland from the Firth of Forth. Mary insisted on riding beside the King as they rode through the city as large crowds cheered their princess on her way, escorted by a large contingent of pipes and drums that almost drowned out the cheers. Bringing up the rear rode

Catesby and Lovell and their attendants who would travel to York with the princess and then present her to Richard.

On reaching the outskirts of Berwick - Upon - Tweed, Mary was overcome with emotion as she bade a final farewell to her family and to Scotland as she prepared to enter England through the gates of Berwick seated in her litter decorated with the arms of Scotland and of England embroidered with gold thread on a scarlet velvet background, with her children seated beside her.

The day that Richard secretly dreaded dawned with a pale sun struggling to break through a cloudy sky above the city of York. He sighed as Tom Murgatroyd, his usual cheerful self, appeared ready to shave his King. He placed a warm towel around Richard's shoulders then began to shave him.

'A big day fer thee today, Sire' He began. ' I'll get thee to look tha best fer t'lady'

'I'm sure you will, Tom' Richard lapsed into silence staring into space as Tom chattered on until he too fell silent, realizing that the King was not in a talkative mood.

The shave completed, Richard crossed the chamber to where two of his squires waited to assist his dressing.

Shortly afterwards he was joined for breakfast by Sir Richard Ratcliffe, Sir Ralph de Assheton and Sir Robert Percy.


Princess Mary also was unusually apprehensive that morning as her maids dressed her in a new gown then braided her hair before adding the final touch, a matching headdress in the latest hood style. Just after midday the princess and her unusually subdued children, entered her litter and accompanied by her escort party of ladies, gentlemen, musicians and men at arms, set off on the final part of their epic journey through the forest of Galtres which led almost to the gates of York. An hour later Richard, mounted on White Surrey, together with his company, left his lodgings at the Austin Friars and rode in procession to the West Door of York's impressive Minster where he would greet his future Queen. From the West Door he had a clear view of the northern entrance to the city at Bootham Bar through which Princess Mary would shortly pass through. Richard gravely acknowledged the greetings of the Archbishop, the Lord

Mayor and the City Fathers as he reined in White Surrey and took his place at the front of the assembled company.

Not long afterwards the trumpeters standing on the walls on either side of Bootham Bar, raised their instruments and sounded a fanfare as the Scottish party came into view. This was the signal for the bells of the Minster to ring out their welcome. Gradually, another sound unfamiliar to English ears, drew everyone's attention as the Scottish procession entered the city led by Piper's and Drummers beating out a tune. Immediately behind them pulled by four matching white ponies, came the Royal Litter with its curtains tied back so that all the people could see her, sat the Princess Mary with her children beside her.

As the litter came to a halt facing the Minster, the wintry sun suddenly burst from behind a cloud flooding the scene with light as Richard dismounted from his horse and began to walk slowly towards the litter. Both Catesby and Lovell who had ridden just behind the princess and were on hand to assist her and the children. Princess Mary stood upright, her left hand clutching that of her daughter and with her son standing on her right, her outward composure belying her frantically beating heart as she watched the king drawing closer.

'Now, children' She dropped to the ground in a deep curtsey with her eyes lowered that took in the king's black boots

'Please rise, my Lady ' Richard took her hand in his and raised it to his lips as she slowly arose from her curtsey. They were both momentarily startled as their eyes met for the first time when Richard continued in his warm musical voice.

'I bid you most welcome to York, my lady '

'I, I thank your grace' Quickly recovering herself.

'I am very happy to be here' Mary replied with a small smile.

As she looked up at Richard she was relieved to see that Catesby and Lovell had not lied about the king's pleasing appearance. She was immediately impressed by his handsome face framed by his shoulder length, slightly wavy hair topped by his dark blue velvet hat on which glittered a sapphire and diamond white boar badge. His outfit was completed by a long blue cloak lined with black fur over which he wore a heavy chain of linked white Yorkist sunnes and roses.

42

Richard in turn, looked closely at the Princess for the first time and saw a young woman with a pleasing heart shaped face with blue eyes framed by her green and white velvet hood that showed a glimpse of her rich auburn hair. She was slim but shapely built and just came up to his shoulder in height.

'May I present my children to your grace?' She asked softly.

Richard nodded and turned to the little boy who bowed low then treated the King to a broad grin.

'My son, Lord Robert Hamilton and my daughter, Lady Elizabeth.'

'I am delighted to meet you, children ' He smiled as little Elizabeth, overcome by shyness, hid her face in her mother's gown. The hovering nursemaid then stepped forward and with a curtsey, led them away as Richard offered his hand to Mary and led her into the Minster to give thanks for her safe arrival.

When the short service was over, he led her back to the litter where the children awaited them. He then mounted White Surrey ready to escort them on the short ride to their lodgings at nearby St Mary's Abbey.

Leaning out of the litter, Robert exclaimed excitedly, ' Och, Sire, what a bootiful horse'

'Robert, remember to whom you speak ' Mary grabbed her son and hauled him back onto his seat. 'I must apologise for my son's ill manners, your grace ' She spoke flushing contritely.

'No harm done, my Lady' Richard replied gently.' And yes, young Sir, White Surrey *is* a beautiful Horse ' He said turning to the Robert

'Would you like a ride upon him? '

'Och aye, please, Sire' The little boy's face lit up in delight as a man at arms lifted him up and placed him in front of Richard on the horse's broad back to the cheers of the bystanders, the procession then set off in the direction of St Mary's Abbey.

When Mary and the children were finally settled in their comfortably furnished chambers, Richard took Mary's hand in his and kissing her finger tips, bade her farewell telling her.

'My Lady, I look forward to our next meeting before the high altar in the Minster on the day after tomorrow when you will do me the honour of becoming my wife and my Queen '

'Your grace ' Mary replied, ' The honour is all mine' And swept him a deep curtsey as he turned to leave.

# 10

The day of the royal wedding dawned bright but with a chilly breeze. The ceremony was due to commence in the Minster at ten o'clock in the morning followed by a celebratory dinner in the city's Guildhall before the royal couple left York for the ten mile journey to Richard's castle at Sheriff Hutton.

Both bride and groom rose early to prepare for the momentous day ahead. Richard was in a decidedly edgy mood as Tom Murgatroyd helped him to bathe and to dress in his sumptuous outfit of cloth of gold edged with purple and red velvet and topped by a matching floor length cloak lined with ermine. Across his shoulders he wore his golden collar decorated with the Yorkist Sunnes and Roses and hanging from the centre was his personal device of the White Boar flashing with diamonds whenever he moved. At last Tom stood back admiring his handiwork.

'By 'eck, Sire. Tha looks a fair treat even if I do say it mesen'

'Thank you, Tom. Let's just get through today' he answered wryly.

In the adjoining chamber his closest friends awaited him, equally bedecked in their finest array except for Francis Lovell who was dressed in the deepest black out of respect for his recently deceased wife. He approached Richard and asked him quietly.

'Are you ready, Dickon. The Princess seems like a kindly lady?'

'As ready as I will ever be' He replied forcing a smile. 'Gentlemen, come, the Minster awaits '

In the guest quarters of St Mary's Abbey, the activity reached fever pitch as Princess Mary's personal maid, Jeanie McColl, added the final touches to her mistress's wedding gown by fastening a beautiful necklace of diamonds in the shape of Roses around her slender neck that brought gasps of admiration from the other ladies present. 'Will I pass muster, Jeanie?' Mary asked anxiously.

'Oh aye, my Lady. king Richard will be bowled over when he claps eyes on you'

Jeanie McColl was a forty year old widow whose late husband had been killed in the service of Mary's first husband, Lord Hamilton, eight years earlier during a skirmish in the highlands.

'I hope so, Jeanie. I want to do justice to the king's magnificent wedding gift,' Mary answered.

Richard had sent his gift to her by a trusted courier the day before.

A fanfare of trumpets almost drowned out the sound of the bells and the cheers of the crowds as Richard entered the Minster and made his way slowly towards the altar as the organ played a welcoming air. The large congregation made up of his relatives, members of the nobility and the Lord Mayor and Aldermen of the City of York, rose to its feet and bowed and curtseyed as he passed by them. The Archbishop of York stood before the Altar and stepping forward raised his hand in blessing as Richard knelt and crossed himself. Upon rising he stood waiting for what seemed like an awful long time to him, but was in reality, only ten minutes before the trumpets sounded the arrival of his bride as Mary, her hand on the arm of her little son, began her long slow walk down the aisle towards him.

They stood side by side and turned simultaneously to glance at each other. Mary gave an involuntary gasp at Richard's appearance topped by his glittering golden crown. He in turn, to his surprise, couldn't help but be impressed by Mary's splendid wedding attire. Her gown was of heavy satin in the colours of Scotland. The blue Saltire of St Andrew on a white background, that began at the waist and fell to the hem on both the front and on the back of the garment. Her headdress of blue and white stripes was also made of satin with a long blue veil edged with white which fell to the ground in graceful folds.

The Congregation was silent as the Nuptial Mass commenced. Richard made his vows in a clear voice followed by Mary who made her responses in her customary low key Scottish accent. Finally, the Archbishop pronounced them man and wife. To the sound of the organ playing a joyous Te Deum, the king led his new Queen by the hand back down the aisle to the great West Door there to be greeted by the cheers of the crowds waiting outside. The wintry sun burst through the clouds and the bells of all the city churches rang out as Richard and Mary began the short walk to the nearby Guildhall for the lavish banquet, a gift from the City of York.

The newly wedded Sovereigns walked slowly, acknowledging the enthusiastic greetings of the crowds of well-wishers lining the route so by the time they reached their destination. Their guests, who took a different route, were awaiting them in the great hall. They entered to a fanfare of trumpets and took their throne like seats on the raised dais.

As the lavish meal progressed, Richard noticed that Mary was eating very little, pushing her food around her trencher.

'Is the food not to your liking, my lady? ' He asked.

'Oh, it isn't that, my lord ' she answered flushing. 'It is just that today has been so, so exceptional that I fear it has cost me my appetite '

'I too must confess that I am not very hungry ' Smiling ruefully, Richard continued. 'But, as we must commence our journey to Sheriff Hutton shortly, I think it would be wise to try and eat something to keep up our strength '

'You are quite right of course, my lord ' Mary nodded and with a shy smile, scooped up a piece of juicy meat and popped it into her mouth.

After the feast ended they retired to separate chambers to change from their wedding finery into warm travelling clothes. Although the day was fine for the time of year, it would grow colder as the daylight began to fade so the need for warm apparel was vital.

When they finally emerged from the Guildhall Richard was surprised when Mary, instead of entering her litter, began to mount a richly caparisoned black Stallion.

'You are riding, my lady? ' He questioned, with a slight frown.

'Yes, if it please you, my Lord. Black Laddie needs the exercise and I am sorely in need of some fresh air. I find the litter somewhat stifling '

'Then we will ride together, my lady, and I will point out places of interest on our way' Richard glanced uneasily as Mary's horse started to prance when she was in the saddle but she calmed him down immediately and by the time that they had left York behind he realised that she was a superb horsewoman.


It was dusk as the cavalcade approached Sheriff Hutton Castle and men –at-arms stood on either side of the path leading to the drawbridge holding aloft blazing braziers to light their way. Once over the drawbridge and inside the inner courtyard, Mary noted the four square towers joined by various buildings before Richard led her up a stone staircase and into the great Hall of the keep lit by hundreds of candles and the blazing fires from the two enormous fireplaces located at both ends of the room..

They were followed by Mary's two children who had travelled by litter together with their nursemaid. The children, weary from their journey, were quickly taken to their bed chamber there to be fed and settled for the night while Richard introduced Mary to his assorted relatives led by his nephew and present heir, John de la Pole, Earl of Lincoln, a tall young man of twenty three, the son of his sister Elizabeth, Duchess of Suffolk, who knelt and kissed the Queen's hand.

He was followed by Margaret and Edward of Warwick. Margaret curtseyed deeply but much to her chagrin, Edward cried out, 'Is this lady now a Queen, my lord uncle?'

'Yes, Edward,' Richard answered trying not to laugh. 'So you must bow, then kneel and kiss her grace's hand '

Looking suitably chastened, Edward blushed a fiery red and knelt but before he could kiss her hand, Mary reached out and drew the little boy into her arms saying softly, 'I am your aunt Mary, Edward. I'm sure that we will become great friends.'

She signalled for Margaret to come forward to join her brother then kissed both children gently.

'I like aunt Mary, my lord uncle,' Edward called to Richard much to everyone's amusement.

Next to be presented were Richard's five nieces, the daughters of his late brother, Edward IV led by the eldest, Elizabeth.

'Lady Elizabeth,' exclaimed Mary. 'You are every bit as beautiful as I was led to believe.'

'Your grace is very kind,' Elizabeth murmured as she arose from her curtsey to receive Mary's kiss on her cheek.

The last members of Richard's family to be introduced caused a few whispered comments and looks of surprise on the faces of the assembled courtiers that were quickly suppressed as Richard announced.

'My lady, I present to you my natural son and daughter, Sir John of Pontefract and Katherine, the wife of William Herbert, earl of Huntingdon.'

With one graceful movement, John knelt and kissed Mary's hand and she was amazed to see how much the young man resembled his father in appearance with his brown hair and his blue-grey eyes. Katherine also shared the same family resemblance.

As she rose from her obeisance Mary couldn't help but notice that sixteen year old Katherine was quite well advanced in pregnancy.

'Why, my lord,' Mary turned to Richard with a smile. 'I had no idea that you will shortly become a grandfather'

'Life is full of surprises, my lady,' Richard replied softly, returning her smile.

It had been a long day and both Richard and Mary were feeling equally apprehensive in their different ways about the day's final ceremony. The traditional bedding when the bride and groom would be publicly put to bed in the presence of the wedding guests as the archbishop sprinkled the bed with holy water and blessed the newly wedded couple.

This ceremony usually ended with lots of laughter and crude jokes, especially if the guests had had plenty to drink. Anticipating this, Richard had ordered that apart from the genuine good wishes, there was to be no lewd behaviour. As he had said earlier to his friend, 'It's not as if this is a first marriage for either the Queen or for myself.'

Mary, wearing a richly embroidered nightgown, was attended by the ladies of the court, as she entered the royal bedchamber first and climbed into the sumptuous four poster bed and sat upright against the piled up pillows. When Richard entered, accompanied by his grinning gentlemen, he climbed into the bed and sat beside her. The Archbishop of York, who stood waiting at the bed's foot, then made the sign of the cross as he blessed the royal couple before signalling to the chattering courtiers to follow him from the chamber, quietly closing the door behind them.

Alone at last, Richard turned to look closely at Mary as if for the first time. He gasped inwardly as Mary's beauty enhanced by the flickering candles, hit him. He reached out and gently stroked her rippling auburn hair.

'You are truly lovely, my lady,' he whispered in an awed voice.

'And you, Sire, are an amazing man,' Mary breathed as Richard drew her into his arms.

# 11

Waking suddenly, Mary realised that Richard was no longer beside her and that it was still the middle of the night as the darkness still held sway through the slits in the curtains. As her eyes grew accustomed to the gloom she noticed that Richard was sitting by the light of a single candle at a table with his head in his hands before the dying embers of the fire.

Sitting upright she shivered as the chill air made her shiver again. Climbing out of the bed she slid her feet into her fur line slippers and donned her woollen cloak and secured it about herself. Seeing that Richard was clad only in his thin night shirt, she picked up his fur lined cloak that had lain beside her own and approached him so quietly that he wasn't aware of her presence until she stood beside him.

'Are you feeling ill, my lord? ' Mary asked anxiously. 'Forgive me for disturbing you but you must be frozen stiff sitting here with the fire going out.'

Before he could answer, she had placed his cloak around his shoulders.

'Thank you, my lady. I hope that I didn't waken you and no, I am not ill.'

'Perhaps something is troubling you then, my lord. If you would like to talk I'm told that I am a very good listener.' She smiled. 'I am also very discreet '

Richard waived her to the seat opposite him then stood to wrap the cloak fully around him before bending to poke some life back into the dying fire. He resumed his seat, and smiling ruefully, started to explain

'I couldn't sleep because my conscience was troubling me. You will probably think it strange, but I felt that I had betrayed my late

50

wife by re-marrying and finding you, my new wife, so irresistible.' He paused, shaking his head. 'You must find me quite odd '

Mary looked at him gravely before replying. 'On the contrary, my lord, I understand your dilemma only too well because I also felt quite guilty at the thought of re – marrying '

'Then you loved your late husband?'

'I gradually grew to love him and to respect him but I was never in love with him.' Mary paused and a faraway look came into her eyes. 'I will try and explain. I was a very young and giddy lassie when my marriage to Lord James Hamilton was arranged. I was appalled at the thought of marrying a man forty years older than I who had a son older than me. I pleaded with my brother, the King, but to no avail. He needed the Hamilton clans support against the Douglas faction who were on the warpath yet again '

Richard sat with his hand resting on his chin as he listened intently.

'But you grew to love him?'

'Aye, but it took a long time before I realised what a good man he was. He was very kind and patient with me and he gave me two beautiful bairns.'

'So you understand how I am feeling?' Richard nodded.

'Aye, my lord .But it is much worse for you because I have been led to believe that yours was a true love match.'

'Yes ' Mused Richard. 'Anne and I had known each other since we were children growing up in her father's castle at Middleham in Wensleydale, which is not very far from here. Her father was the then powerful earl of Warwick and I had been sent to Middleham as a young lad to learn how to become skilled in arms and knightly manners. A few years later after I had returned to my brother's court. Warwick defected to the Lancastrians and I didn't see Anne again for a very long time. Her father married her off to the so called Lancastrian Prince of Wales in France and I was in despair. But, events moved on until Warwick was killed at the battle of Barnet just before the Lancastrian army landed in the west country, led by Anne's husband and her mother-in- law from Hell, Margaret of Anjou and tagging reluctantly along with them, my Anne. Our armies met at Tewkesbury and my brothers, king Edward and

George of Clarence and I won the day which left Anne a fifteen year old widow'

Edward sent her to live with George and his wife, Isabel, who was Anne's elder sister. I met up with Anne and we fell in love with each other. Edward gave his consent to our marriage but George objected because the sisters were co - heiresses to the lands and fortunes that Warwick had originally acquired through his marriage to their mother, a great heiress. So long as Anne remained unwed, George had control of the lot. When he learned of our plans, he hid Anne away in a cook shop in the city. I searched high and low for her and thanks to a tip off, I eventually found her and we married soon afterwards then moved north to make our home at Middleham, the place that held so many happy memories for us.'

Richard paused and with a sigh continued. ' We were very happy there, especially when our son, Edward, was born. Edward died suddenly almost two years ago, just a few weeks short of his tenth birthday. What made it even harder for us to bear was the fact that Anne and I were not with him, we were in Nottingham at the time'

His voice wavering, Richard continued, 'My poor Anne had always been frail, as was our little Edward. She knew that she would never conceive another child and that certainty devastated her, she was keenly aware that as king I needed an heir of my body. However hard I tried to reassure her that her health was more important to me than anything else, but she began to slowly die after our son was buried. She began to cough blood and eventually the Physicians advised me to shun her bed for by then she was in a highly infectious state. But how could I abandon her? I couldn't.' Richard's voice dropped to a whisper as he relived the horror of that time. 'I just couldn't.'

Mary, with tears in her eyes, reached out across the table and pressed his hand. 'I am so very sorry,' she said quietly. 'I can only begin to imagine how difficult it must be for you to tell me, a virtual stranger all of this. But I thank you and hope that we can become friends.'

'I am sure that we will be,' he answered. Then with a change of mood said, 'Let us begin by you calling me Richard when we are in private, Mary.'

'Gladly, Richard.' She smiled. 'My family call me Marie, after my mother.'

'Marie it shall be then,' Richard raised himself from his chair and held out his hand saying. 'Come, Marie, it grows decidedly chilly now that the fire has finally died. Let us return to our bed where we will be much more comfortable'

Halfway across the chamber they were stopped in their tracks by a frantic scratching at the door followed by a plaintive howling and more scratching.

'What is that dreadful noise?' Mary whispered clutching the neck of her robe.

'I know what it is' Richard strode to the door and flinging it open was almost knocked off his feet by an ecstatic Rex who flung himself at his master in his customary orgy of tail wagging and licks while Mary looked on in amazement.

'Sit, Rex' Richard disentangled himself and pointed to the ground. Reluctantly, the large hound slumped to the floor, his tail still wagging as Richard turned to Mary saying.

'I hope that you like dogs, Marie '

'Aye I do, and have brought one from Scotland with me but Wee Hamish, who sleeps in the bairns chamber, is nothing like the size of this laddie ' She stepped forward and gingerly held out her hand for Rex to sniff before asking Richard,

'Will this big laddie allow me to stroke him? '

'Oh yes,' Richard answered, relieved that Mary appeared to be at ease with dogs. 'Rex is everyone's friend '

And to prove it, Rex began to lick her hand while with her other hand, she stroked his head and tickled him beneath his chin.

Later, as Richard and Mary settled down in the bed, Rex decided to join them and with a great leap landed at their feet and began to make himself comfortable until Richard dragged him off by his collar with the command to, ' STAY THERE ' and pointed to the floor strewed with sweet smelling rushes. 'AND DO NOT MOVE AGAIN.'

Which Mary thought was a hilarious ending to a memorable day.

# 12

It was the day before Christmas Eve and the castle servants were working on the final preparations for the coming celebrations with much cleaning and the laying of sweet smelling rushes on the floors. And the cutting down of the gigantic Yule Log that would burn steadily in the great Hall for the festive twelve days. The hall was also decorated by hanging branches of both Holly and Ivy and more discreetly, by sprigs of Mistletoe.

In the corners sat the Tailors and the Seamstresses, their nimble fingers stitching new clothes. But the busiest of all were the Cooks and Scullions, sweating in the heat of the great kitchens as they made their preparations for all the feasting.

Outside the snow was steadily falling, growing deeper as the hours passed. It was so bad that Mary's children, Robert and Elizabeth along with young Edward of Warwick, were forced to play indoors instead of in the gardens.

They ran riot round the hall, screaming with laughter and throwing a ball to four other young players, children of castle workers whom they had befriended, and oblivious to the muttered curses of the men and women trying to do their jobs despite the disruption. Causing even more mayhem were Rex, the King's dog, who had made great friends with the children and also with Wee Hamish, a small white Scottish terrier who had accompanied his mistress the Queen, on her journey from Scotland. Who despite his small size, was quite capable of holding his own in an argument as the much larger castle dogs had soon discovered.

The rumpus soon brought Tom Murgatroyd hurrying as fast as his limp would allow him, in to the hall followed almost immediately by Mary's maid Jeanie McColl, who clapping her hands for silence cried,

'Ye bairns, cease this din right now and come awa wi me tay your rooms'

And turning to Tom said in a voice that brooked no argument.

'Get that great beastie of yours out of here, Master Murgatroyd afore he does some damage ye ken'

'Aye, Mistress McColl' replied Tom as out of breath, he finally managed to grab Rex and to slip his leash over his head.


In his daytime chamber on the floor above, Richard sat at his desk reading and signing state papers attended by his secretary, John Kendall, when they were interrupted by his gentleman usher.

'Well, What is it?' Richard asked impatiently. 'Cannot you see that we are busy?'

'I beg your grace's pardon 'The man bowed ' But a courier has arrived with an urgent message for your grace from London '

Richard sighed and threw down his quill, and bade the courier to be brought before him. The courier entered, wrapped from head to foot in a heavy cloak that dripped melting snow onto the rich carpet forming an unsightly puddle as he knelt before Richard and produced from deep within an inner pocket a missive bearing the seal of Sir Robert Brackenbury, governor of the Tower of London

'Do you know the content Of this message? '

'No, your grace ' answered the man through teeth chattering with the cold. 'I am merely the courier'

'Very well' Richard turned to the usher, 'See to it that this man has some hot food and a change into dry clothing '

'At once, your grace '

Both men bowed and withdrew from the chamber but Richard scarcely noticed their departure, so engrossed was he by the message from Sir Robert Brackenbury, who had fought beside him at Bosworth and whom he trusted implicitly. He read it through twice before ordering Kendall to summon his friends and councillors to attend him immediately.

Lovell was the first to arrive, quickly followed by all the others. 'What is it, Dickon?' He asked with the familiarity of their long friendship.

'I have received some great news, gentlemen.' Beamed Richard. 'The arch traitor Morton escaped somehow from Barnard Castle but has been recaptured, trying to take ship from Lynn. But thanks to a keen eyed Innkeeper who recognised him, he was apprehended and Brackenbury now holds him secure in the Tower and awaits our further instructions '

The assembled men turned to each other muttering in amazement and grinning broadly. John Morton was the currant bishop of Ely and a staunch Lancastrian supporter. For years he had secretly plotted with Margaret Beaufort to remove the Yorkist claimants to the throne and to replace them with Margaret's son, Henry Tudor who lived in exile in Brittany.

His devious mind saw advancement in the church if he succeeded in placing Tudor on the throne. He had been promised the see of Canterbury followed hopefully by being created a cardinal by the Pope. After being implicated in the plot against Richard when he was Lord Protector, the plot that had cost Richard's supposed friend, Lord Hastings, his life. Richard had sent him as a prisoner of his friend, the Duke of Buckingham to his home, Brecknock castle in Wales where clever Morton played on the weak Buckingham's vanity, promising him that he would support *his* weak claim to the throne if he would raise a rebellion against Richard. The rising failed and Buckingham lost his head while the cunning Morton seized his chance and fled overseas to join Tudor in Brittany.

Richard stood with both hands on his hips, searching the faces of the men standing before him.

'Well gentlemen, what action should I now take with Morton? I would welcome your suggestions '

The answers came fast and furiously from cries of 'Execute him' 'Put him on trial' to 'dump him in a dungeon and let him rot.'

Richard raised his hand for silence then turned to Catesby who had stood silently with a thoughtful expression on his face while those around him had shouted out their raucous suggestions.

'You are very quiet, Will, what do *you* think I should do? '

Catesby cleared his throat before answering calmly. ' I think, your grace, that for all his undoubted villainy, and because despite that, he is a high ranking churchman, we must not act hastily in this matter as Morton is subject to canon law and we cannot afford to offend holy church '

Richard nodded slowly in agreement. his mood matching Catesby's sober one.

'You are right of course, Will. We must proceed carefully'

He was interrupted by Ralph de Assheton who suggested with a wink.

'Suppose he met with an accident?. The traitor is not a young man and could easily trip on a flight of stairs, your grace '

Richard had to laugh at de Assheton's assumed air of innocence before continuing.

'As the festive season is now almost upon us, I cannot take any action until after Twelfth Night. So I will think on this matter and inform you of my decision anon' He nodded in dismissal before resuming his seat at his desk.

# 13

It was approaching midnight on Christmas Eve. The snow had ceased falling earlier in the day and the clear sky was lit by hundreds of twinkling stars and a full moon shone down as the entire household at Sheriff Hutton led by the King and Queen, warmly wrapped in furs against the bitter cold, led the way to the chapel across the courtyard, their feet crunching on the icebound path, to celebrate the Mass of the Nativity.

Afterwards, back in the great Hall of the castle they were welcomed by goblets of hot mulled wine and everyone began to exchange Christmas greetings with each other.

The excited children were hurried off, under protests to their beds by their nursemaids, leaving the adults to laugh and to joke amongst themselves until Richard clapped his hands for silence before bidding everyone to,

'Accept Yuletide greetings from myself and from my lady, the Queen. Now, be off to your beds and a good night's sleep for tomorrow, or I should say, today, will be a hectic one'

Taking Mary by the hand he led her to their bed chamber whispering, 'I have a special gift for you, Marie my love '

'Oh, Richard, whatever can that be ? '

She murmured squeezing his hand as he dismissed their waiting attendants.

Later, in the morning, Richard and Mary graciously received many and varied gifts from the assembled company and they in turn distributed gifts to all the children, relatives, and to favoured courtiers. Even the dogs, Rex and Wee Hamish were given new collars to wear.

After a brief respite in the afternoon came the highlight of the day. The Christmas banquet when the sound of trumpets heralded the arrival in the great Hall of the king and Queen, sumptuously arrayed in regal splendour and glittering with jewels, took their place on the throne like chairs in the centre of the high table where Richard signalled for the feast to begin.

And what a feast it was. Richard and Mary were served on bended knee with a choice from so many courses it was difficult to choose a dish that ranged from Venison, roasts of Beef, Pork, in a rich gravy to various types of fish like Salmon, Eels, Bream, Lampreys, Pike, Trout and even exotic sea fish like the Porpoise.

Also included were Oysters and Lobsters. There were also birds ranging in size from a Peacock arrayed in all its feathers, to the tiniest of Sparrows. And to finish, an enormous choice of sweetmeats made from a variety of Nuts, Cakes made with Marzipan and Jellies made from seasoned Fruits, All liberally washed down with fine wines or ale. While all the guests feasted, the Musicians in the gallery played favourite and seasonal tunes while the whole proceedings were presided over by the traditional Lord of Misrule who this Christmas was represented in the person of Davie, a young chef from the castle kitchens.

When the feasting came to an end and the tables were removed, Davie announced that the fun would now begin and that the lords and ladies must remember to obey him in all things.

He organised games for the children like Hunt the Slipper and a Donkey race which involved many of the lord's losing their dignity as they crawled on their hands and knees with a youngster astride their back urging them on while holding a carrot dangling from a stick before them.

The delighted winner of that particular game was Edward of Warwick riding on the back of a puffing duke of Norfolk. Other guests were summoned by Davie to sing or to tell stories. Sir Ralph de Assheton began telling a particularly bawdy tale until he was tapped on the shoulder by the wand of the Lord of Misrule and told to keep the tale clean as there were ladies and children present. Duly reprimanded, de Assheton ended his story on a suitably subdued note to much laughter.

He was followed by Jugglers and Acrobats and various Minstrels after which Davie approached Francis Lovell who had sat quietly watching all the antics. Because it was a festive occasion, Lovell had laid aside his mourning black and was finely dressed in a matching doublet and hose of light grey. He looked momentarily surprised when the Lord of Misrule bowed before him holding out a lute.

'Pray give us a song, my lord. I'm told that you have a reet gradely voice '

As he hesitated, encouraging shouts and whistles resounded from his highly amused friends so he took the lute from Davie's outstretched hand and got to his feet facing the high table saying,

'Here goes then '

And he began to sing a popular ballad about Robin Hood in a strong voice with everyone joining him in the chorus. As he sang, Mary glanced down the table to where she was surprised to see both a rapt and an adoring expression on the face of Richard's niece, Elizabeth. She smiled to herself thinking, 'Ah, so that's the way the wind is blowing. Bess could do far worse for herself than Lovell who was both handsome *and* wealthy''

His song finished, Lovell, grinning broadly acknowledged the cheers and applause from his friends and handed the lute back to the hovering Davie who to everyone's amazement, turned and approached the high table.

Shaking with nerves, Davie knelt before Mary and asked her in a trembling voice, 'Would your grace please do us the great honour of singing for us? '

There was a momentary stunned silence then the hall erupted into cries of, 'Aye, your grace,' and 'Twill be our special Christmas treat.'

Looking at a smiling Richard for his approval, she then held out her hand for the lute saying, 'I must obey the Lord of Misrule so I will sing you a merry Scottish song. '

The company listened in amazed silence as Mary's voice soared up and around the hall accompanied by her skilled playing on the lute. They had heard rumours about her skilled musicianship but had never experienced it before. When the last note faded away, they rose to their feet *en masse* cheering and stamping their feet and repeated pleas of

'More, your grace'

Holding up her hand for silence she announced, 'I thank you very much and will give you one more song. This time one that you will all know, my favourite Christmas air, 'Lullay My Child.'

Gesturing towards Lovell she said, 'My lord Lovell, join me if you please.'

Lovell looking somewhat sheepish came to stand beside her then his tenor and her soprano voices rang out in unison, moving some people, including Richard, almost to tears with the beauty of the words and melody.

With the applause still ringing in their ears, Lovell bowed and kissed her hand then led Mary back to her seat beside Richard.

When the tumult had finally died down. The Lord of Misrule announced, 'Your  graces, my lords, ladies and gentlemen. The dancing will now commence if you can get up off your backsides after stuffing your gobs with all that grub'

The music struck up a rhythmic tune as Richard and Mary led the way to the floor quickly followed by more and more couples. For the next dance Richard partnered his niece, Elizabeth while Lovell partnered Mary. Halfway through the dance, Mary suddenly stopped opposite Richard and Elizabeth saying to Richard, 'I am sorry but I am feeling a little faint, my lord. Will you please escort me back to my chair? Perhaps you will continue with the Lady Elizabeth, my lord Lovell?'

'It will be my pleasure, your grace,' Lovell bowed and smiling, took Elizabeth's hand.

Once back in their seats, Richard asked with a puzzled expression on his face.

'What was all that about?'

'Oh, You men' Mary replied shaking her head 'You just do not see what is staring you in your face, do you. Did you not notice the rapt expression on Elizabeth's face when Francis was singing? She is clearly besotted with him '

'With Frank?'

Richard exclaimed as Mary's revelation slowly dawned on him, 'You know, you could be right. I noticed that she blushed when he bade her good morning recently.'

Mary tapped her chin thoughtfully.

'She could do far worse, Richard. Francis is both handsome and wealthy and, more importantly, he is utterly loyal to you.'

'Aye , he is all those things *and* he is in need of an heir.'

His eyes twinkled as he patted her hand. 'Thank you, Marie my dear. I will sound him out without delay on this matter '

The dance had ended and Lovell and Elizabeth sat down together.

'Ah look at Bess,' Richard exclaimed as he watched the happy smile on his niece's face as Lovell said something amusing that made her laugh.

'Lovell cannot be blind to that adoring look '

'Perhaps he is too recently widowed to think about another marriage?' considered Mary.

'His marriage was not a happy one,' Richard replied. 'When they were wed they were only children and as they grew up they realised that they had absolutely nothing in common with each other. Perhaps he could find happiness with a lovely lass like Bess.'

# 14

The feeling that the coming spring was in the air was very strong on a day during the first week in March 1486. The fields around Sherriff Hutton were bursting with Buttercups and the steep slopes that led down to the castle moat were carpeted in a colourful array of purple, yellow and white crocuses. The day, Tuesday, began like any other day with no hint of the shattering news to come that would devastate Richard.

The Castle hummed with the usual daily activities. The Archer's practising at the butts, Laundresses taking advantage of the fine sunny morning by hanging out the washing to dry, while the Blacksmith and his apprentice sweated from the heat in the forge as they shod one of the large war horses.

The children were at their lessons and Mary and her ladies sat at their needlework while one of the ladies read aloud to them from a book of French romances.

Lady Elizabeth was no longer one of Mary's ladies. She was now Viscountess Lovell since she and Francis Lovell had married ten days previously in a quiet ceremony in the castle chapel. Leaving immediately afterwards on the long journey south to Minster Lovell, the Lovell family seat which was quite close to the city of Oxford.

True to his word soon after Christmas, Richard had spoken to Lovell about the possibility of a match between him and Lady Elizabeth.

'Dickon, are you serious about this? '

He had asked Richard wide eyed with amazement.

' I am indeed, Frank ' Richard had answered.

'For two very good reasons. Firstly, I need to wed Bess to someone that I can trust. I cannot allow the possibility of her marrying another Tudor like candidate and secondly, the lass is clearly in love with you '

' In love with me? I had no idea'

Lovell shook his head in bewilderment.

'You must be the only person in the whole castle not to have noticed the adoring looks she throws at you,' laughed Richard.

'But seriously, Frank, will you give the matter some serious consideration? '

Lovell nodded. 'I know that I must re –marry and I would be honoured to wed the Lady Elizabeth...' He paused for a moment then suddenly burst out laughing.

'What do you find so amusing?' Richard asked.

Still laughing uproariously, Lovell wiped his eyes before answering. 'Have just realised, Dickon, that if I wed lady Bess, I will have to call you uncle.'


Richard had just returned from a hunting expedition on that spring like morning and was taking some midday refreshment with Mary when a messenger arrived at the castle begging an immediate audience with the King. The messenger was brought before him and Richard felt a sense of foreboding as the man, dressed entirely from head to foot in black, relieved only by the badge of the earl of Huntingdon on his tunic, knelt before him.

'Speak up, man. Give me your news.'

He commanded in an unusually harsh voice.

'I regret that I bring your grace sad tidings. Eight days ago, your grace's daughter, Lady Katherine died in childbirth at Raglan Castle in Wales.'

Richard took a step backwards, almost stumbling with shock as Mary reached out to steady him.

'Does the child live?'

'No, your grace. The child, a son, was born dead. Lady Katherine's husband, my lord of Huntingdon, is inconsolable and sends his grace this missive.'

Mary took the sealed letter that he held out.

'His grace and I thank you for bringing this sad news. You may leave us now.'

The man, relieved that he had delivered the message, arose, bowed and hastily quit the chamber.

Richard, with tears in his eyes, took solace in Mary's arms.

'Oh, Marie,' he cried. 'Katherine was only sixteen years old. She was far too young to die. How can I tell her brother? John will take the news very hard. Why do I have to lose everyone that I love.'

'Come my dear,' Mary put her arms around Richard's heaving shoulders and led him to a settle beside the fire. Sitting down beside him, she held him tight while he wept out his shock and sorrow.

After a time his weeping subsided and sitting upright and wiping his eyes, he attempted to smile ruefully.

'I do apologise for my show of weakness, Marie. It will not happen again.'

'There is no need to apologise, Richard, and you are not weak. Far from it. You are one of the strongest men I have ever known and you are entitled to mourn the loss of your dear daughter.'

'Katherine's mother died giving birth to her,' Richard mused. 'Just a year after she had borne John. Her name was Katherine also.'

A faraway look came into his eyes as he looked back into the past.

'She was only a maid servant at Pontefract but despite that, I loved her dearly. We were little more than children ourselves.'

Richard turned to Mary with a smile.

'I don't deserve you, my love. I bless the day that I wed you,' he murmured taking her hand in his.

Mary squeezed his hand and said quietly, 'I also have some news for you, Richard. I am pleased to be able to tell you that I am with child.'

Richard gazed upon her in amazement.

'You are truly with child?'

'Yes, Richard, God willing, you will become a father again come September.'

# 15

By the end of March plans were fully in place to begin the long journey south to London. Richard's prolonged stay in the north had not been spent idly. The Council of the North that he had instigated at Sheriff Hutton before Bosworth was now fully functional with councillors who would keep him fully informed on matters relating to the northern counties of England all the way up to the border with Scotland.

The second of April was a typical spring day, fine with a slight breeze, when the large royal contingent departed from Sheriff Hutton for the ten mile journey to York where they would spend the first night of the journey south.

Much to her chagrin, Mary travelled by litter when Richard had forbidden her to ride her horse.

'I am perfectly capable of riding and it is much more comfortable than the swaying of that damned litter,' she had fumed in one of their rare disagreements.

'Maybe it is,' Richard declared. 'But you are pregnant with the heir to England and you will therefore not risk the horse stumbling and throwing you. You will obey me in this, Mary.'

Glancing at Richard's stern expression, Mary knew that it would be pointless to argue with him and reluctantly allowed him to assist her into the litter.

By the time that they reached York she was feeling too tired to appreciate the glorious display of the masses of Daffodils surrounding the city walls but was glad to be able to stretch out with wee Hamish beside her for the last stretch of the journey, but she wasn't going to admit that to Richard.

It took two more weeks of exhausting travel before the cavalcade finally arrived in London. Two weeks that saw them traverse through all kinds of unpredictable spring weather. Through sunshine, strong winds, and the to be expected April showers when Mary was glad that the hated litter at least saved her from the soakings suffered by her fellow travellers.

She was also fascinated by the diverse countryside, towns and cities like Pontefract, Doncaster, Grantham, Stamford and the final town of any size, Barnet, that they passed through on the two hundred mile trek south. Richard proved to be an excellent guide to his Scottish Queen. Pointing out all the places of interest and telling her the history of the various lodgings where they spent their nights.


Their stay at Pontefract Castle in Yorkshire was especially memorable for Richard. When he had received word that John Morton, the traitorous bishop of Ely had been apprehended trying to flee the country just before Christmas, he had thought long and hard about how he would deal with the conniving prelate.

Under normal circumstances a traitor would be executed by being hung drawn and quartered or at best, beheaded. but Richard was well aware that this could not apply with Morton simply because the man was an ordained priest. If he executed him Richard risked not only excommunication for himself but the placing of the whole country under papal interdict, so he finally decided that he would have Morton moved under heavy guard to lifelong imprisonment in the mighty fortress of Pontefract in west Yorkshire.

He was already installed there when Richard and Mary lodged in the royal apartments for two nights on their way to London. Morton was confined in a small, Spartan chamber in one of the many towers where Richard finally confronted him. He saw before him an elderly man who returned his stare with a mocking smile.

'So, Morton, did you imagine that you would escape me?'

Richard asked in a voice soft but none the less menacing. Morton shrugged before replying.

'Well, now that you have me what are you going to do? For your own soul and for England, you know that you cannot execute me' He smirked.

'No. But I will keep you secure here in this chamber until the day that you die. You will be permitted no visitors or books except the Holy Bible. You will have long to think where your treachery has landed you, and may your sleep be disturbed by the images of my innocent young nephews so cruelly done to death as the result of your plotting'

Richard paused to draw breath before turning to the door before snarling, 'It is my sincerest wish that you will eventually burn in everlasting hell.'

# 16

At every town and village that they passed through Richard and Mary were welcomed by crowds of cheering people who had been informed of their coming by couriers who rode ahead of the main cavalcade. Mary especially was surprised at the warmth of the welcome that she, a stranger to England received, and gratefully accepted the Bunches of flowers and other small gifts offered to her by the young and old alike.

At last London was in sight and even the sun shone for them as at last, they prepared to enter the city through Moorgate.

Richard rode beside Mary who sat upright in the litter, propped up by richly embroidered cushions. The curtains tied back so that all the people could see her. The streets had been swept clean and banners and tapestries hung from the windows of the overhanging buildings. The sound of the accompanying drums and trumpets of the men at arms and all the city church bells pealing out were almost drowned out by the cheering crowds as Richard and Mary were greeted by the Lord Mayor and Aldermen outside St Paul's Cathedral where The Bishop of London also waited to bestow a blessing on the king and Queen.

Much further back in the royal procession, seated atop the leading baggage cart, Jeanie McColl, holding a squirming Wee Hamish on her lap, looked eagerly about her and tried to make herself heard above the din as she turned to Tom Murgatroyd who was struggling to restrain Rex who added to the noise by barking madly.

'Och, Tom, London looks like a braw city.' she shouted.

'Nay, lass' Tom yelled back. 'It is a reet old stinkhole of a place

'Like Edinburgh,' she shouted in reply. 'It's no called Auld Reekie for nothing ye ken.'

Since their work had thrown them together, after a somewhat shaky start, Jeanie and Tom had become good friends through their mutual devotion to Mary and Richard.

'Aye, Jeanie,' he agreed. 'Most towns stink. Give me the countryside every time.'

Once out of the city centre and making their way down the Strand the crowds thinned out but increased in numbers again as the procession approached the Palace of Westminster, a hotch pot of buildings bordered by the River Thames on one side and by the imposing Westminster Abbey on the other whose bells rang out their welcome.

The cavalcade came to a halt outside the entrance to Westminster Hall where the entire court waited to greet their returning King and his new Queen

Richard dismounted from White Surrey, handed the reins to a hovering groom before giving a reassuring smile to a slightly nervous Mary, then leading her by the hand into the hall where to their delight among the assorted group of courtiers waiting to greet them were Francis Lovell and his beaming wife, the lady Elizabeth whom Mary warmly embraced and immediately named her as her Chief lady in waiting.

# 17

Richard and Mary had discussed the matter of her coronation and had decided that it must take place before she went into confinement for the birth of their expected child. The following month, May, was finally chosen for as Mary remarked, patting her slightly swollen belly.

'I don't want to have to waddle to my crowning.'

The day before the coronation Richard escorted Mary by the royal barge down river to the Tower of London where following ancient tradition, she was to spend the night prior to her crowning. The day was overcast with squally showers, cold for the last week in May. As she stepped ashore and entered the precincts of the Tower, Mary looked around her at the imposing buildings, especially the great White Tower that dwarfed its surroundings, as Richard led her to the nearby royal apartments.

'Is this where your young nephews were done to death? '

She asked him with a sudden shudder.

'No, but not far away' Richard replied tight lipped.

'I have had that particular room sealed off. I could not bear to make use of it again'

'I understand, my dear '

Mary murmured patting his hand.

'Forgive me. I should not have mentioned it '

'There is nothing to forgive' Said Richard with a shrug.

'And while we are on the subject, I have had the Beaufort woman removed from here to a nunnery near Barnard Castle in Co Durham. She is of course quite mad and is no longer a threat to the peace of this land'

The Royal apartments were sumptuously furnished and despite her misgivings, Mary slept well in contrast to Richard 's fretful night haunted by troubled memories from the past. They were awakened early the next morning by the sound of church bells heralding the coronation day of the Queen. After being bathed and dressed Richard bade his wife farewell with a kiss as he prepared to leave for Westminster.

'I wish that you could ride beside me this day,' Mary said wistfully as she slid her arms from around his neck.

'Ah, but today is your day, my love, and according to ancient tradition, you must arrive at the Abbey alone' He whispered.

'But do not fear for I and the children will be watching the ceremony from an alcove above the High Altar and afterwards we will be beside you at the coronation banquet in Westminster Hall.'

After what seemed to Mary like hours of preparation. She at last entered her litter and began the journey through the cloudy but thankfully dry city to Westminster. On her arrival Mary's shoes were removed so that she could step bare footed onto the rich Red Carpet that stretched all the way from Westminster Hall to the great West Door of the Abbey where she was greeted by a fanfare of trumpets before she commenced her solemn progress towards the High Alter to the cries of, 'Vivat, Vivat Regina Maria, Vivat Vivat!' from the Choir, followed by the organ bursting into a majestic Te Deum.

The congregation had risen to their feet amid gasps of admiration as the Queen passed them. With her auburn hair worn loose and falling to her waist in waves that caught the light from the stained glass windows, Mary made an impressive figure clad in a gown of shimmering Yellow and Silver cloth of Gold with a low cut square neckline in readiness for the anointing and glittering with jewels. Her heavy Purple velvet train edged with ermine and lined with white Silk, was borne by the Duchess of Norfolk.

Before kneeling as she reached the altar, Mary glanced quickly upwards to where Richard, her awe struck children on either side of him, had followed her progress down the aisle, smiled down at her reassuringly.

The service commenced with the High Mass which was followed immediately by the sacred anointing. Next, the Queen's Coronation Ring was placed on her finger and she received the consort's two Sceptres. Then came the highlight of the ceremony, the placing of the crown upon her head by the Archbishop of Canterbury.

The ritual ended with the Archbishop's blessing before Mary began her return procession along the length of the nave to the thundering sound of the organ accompanying her progress to the West Door wearing her Crown and carrying her Sceptres. On reaching the door, she was helped to step back into her earlier discarded shoes then walked on along the length of the Red carpet into the Palace of Westminster for a much needed respite before the commencement of the banquet.

Immediately after the Queen had passed them by, the waiting crowds descended onto the carpet and there began a scrabble to cut and secure pieces of it to keep as souvenirs until nothing was left except scraps of ruined fabric.

The Coronation Banquet consisting of twenty courses of assorted dishes, each one heralded by a fanfare of Trumpets, began two hours later when the king and Queen, wearing their crowns, entered Westminster Hall and took their throne like seats at the high table after passing through the lines of kneeling assembled courtiers and guests which included a special delegation from Scotland who had been especially invited to witness the crowning of their former Princess as Queen of England

'I was so proud of you today, Marie,' said Richard quietly. 'It must have been exhausting for you in your condition.'

'I confess that I am a wee bit tired.' She smiled in return. 'But I am not ill you know, merely pregnant.'

'Your wife is quite correct, Richard,' interrupted The Duchess of York who sat in a place of honour on her daughter - in - law's left hand side. 'Pregnancy is not an illness. I should know after being brought to bed twelve times myself.'

'I stand corrected, Ma Mere,' laughed Richard shaking his head in amusement at his mother's no nonsense approach.

'But at the same time, Daughter,' she added turning to Mary, 'Do take care of yourself and the heir to England that you carry.'

'Do not worry, Madame,' Mary assured Cecily, 'I have every intention of carrying this pregnancy for full term.'

The two women smiled at each other in perfect understanding. Ever since their first meeting shortly after Mary's arrival in London, a firm bond of friendship had formed between them, each recognising and respecting the other's strength of character.

Despite Mary's refusal to admit it, she was exhausted by the time came to retire for the night.

After dismissing all her ladies, except for Jeanie. She breathed a sigh of relief as she settled herself more comfortably into the large bed.

'Thank you, Jeanie,' she said softly. 'Did you get a good view of the ceremony?'

'Oh aye, my lady, thanks to his grace, Tom Murgatroyd and myself had braw seats. I greeted all the way through it. I was so proud of ye.'

Their conversation was brought to an abrupt end by Richard entering the chamber clad in a woollen floor length robe covering his nightgown.

'Goodnight to you, Jeanie,' he nodded in dismissal as curtseying low, she hurried out closing the chamber door quietly behind her.

'I was so happy for you today, Marie my dear,' whispered Richard as discarding the robe, he climbed into bed and wrapped his arms around her as she snuggled down into his arms.

'Sleep well and god give you sweet dreams,' he kissed her forehead and smiled to himself as he realised that her eyes were already closed and that she was breathing gently as exhaustion finally overcame her.

# 18

As spring turned into summer, rumours of troubles in Scotland between the King and his nobles began to trickle south into England and finally reached London where Richard shrugged off the rumours saying to his councillors that while the Scots argued amongst themselves, they wouldn't be any threat to England

Mary was growing more uneasy as the rumours gathered momentum and confided her fears to Richard who tried to reassure her that her fears were groundless. Then news filtered through that Queen Margaret had tried to persuade king James to at least listen to the Baron's grievances that were many. But it seemed that he had turned on her in a fury and forced her to take up residence in Stirling Castle with the parting words, 'Matters of state are nay women's business,' after accusing her of collusion with the rebel barons and influencing their sons against him.

'Is your brother often given to such rages?' Richard asked Mary.

'Aye, sometimes,' she answered with a nod.

'He is a very indecisive man, a ditherer, who tends to pay too much heed to the latest person who had his ear. And like all weak people, he can be very stubborn.'

The court was resident at Greenwich on what was a sweltering hot 21 July. Mary, in the seventh month of her pregnancy and really feeling the effects of the unaccustomed heat, sat on a trestle beneath a shady tree with her ladies in the gardens that ran down to the banks of the River Thames, trying to keep awake as Bess read to her from a French romance. A serving man approached and kneeling before her offered a cooling drink which she gratefully accepted. Glancing upwards, she saw Richard, accompanied by both Lovell and Catesby, hurrying towards her. Mary, instinctively knowing that they brought bad news, rose unsteadily to her feet, dropping the goblet and spilling its contents over her gown leaving dark stains. At the same time Bess snapped the book shut and reached out to steady Mary just as Richard reached her.

'What is wrong, Richard?' She asked her voice wavering. ' Do you bring bad news? '

'Be seated, my dear', Richard bade, helping her to resume her seat. 'We have received some disturbing news from Scotland concerning your sister – in – law, Queen Margaret. I am very sorry to have to tell you that she died nine days ago at Stirling.'

'Oh no' Mary's hand flew to her mouth in shock. 'Margaret, dead. She was not ill or was she? She was only just thirty years old.'

Richard sat down beside her and clasping her hand firmly in his to steady her, continued, 'No, Marie, she does not appear to have been ill, but earlier in the day the king had visited his wife and according to others present, heated exchanges were overheard between them ending with the King storming out of the chamber dragging his protesting eldest son, James, roughly by the arm and shouting, "You WILL obey me in this, Madame!" as he slammed the chamber door behind him and the young prince who was struggling to break free and crying out, "I do not want to leave you, my lady mother !" and who was in floods of tears.

'The furious red-faced king called for their horses and with an escort of men –at – arms surrounding him and the distraught prince, set off at full gallop bound for Edinburgh— '

Richard stopped in mid-sentence to draw breath, unconsciously tightening his grip on Mary's hand before continuing.

'The Queen then sat down to dinner and about two hours later was violently sick, collapsed and died.'

A stunned silence momentarily followed Richard's news before shocked looks and whispered comments broke out amongst the assembled company.

'Was... was she poisoned?' whispered Mary.

'We do not know for certain,' answered Richard. 'But all kinds of rumours abound. Our couriers will keep us fully informed of any further developments. In the meantime, let us return indoors, my love. You have had a shock and maybe you should lie down for a while.'

'Aye. Perhaps you are right.'

Richard led Mary back into the palace and handed her over to an anxious Jeanie who removed her headdress and helped her onto a day bed where she sat beside her mistress until Mary fell into a troubled sleep.

In the following days more details of the events in Scotland began to emerge. Opinions were divided about whether or not the king was involved in the death of the Queen. Mary received a frenzied letter from her brother in which he denied that he had had any involvement in his wife's death. Shortly afterwards she received another missive, this time from her deeply unhappy thirteen year old nephew, James, who was convinced that his hated father was responsible for his mother's death and swore to avenge her.

Richard and Mary eventually received news from a more reliable source via a courier dispatched by Richard's ambassador in Edinburgh. He confirmed that the country was in turmoil with the Highland Chiefs supporting the king's claim of innocence while the Lowland Lords were convinced of the King's guilt.

'Margaret will be sorely missed,' Mary told Richard. 'She restrained his more erratic and impulsive acts and her dowry brought both the Orkney and the Shetland Islands to be part of Scotland.'

'Let us pray that whatever the truth of this matter may be, that some kind of stability will soon return to your homeland, my love,' replied Richard, leaning over to kiss her cheek. 'That is all that we can hope for at present.'

# 19

Unknown to Mary, Richard ordered the English garrison at Berwick–Upon–Tweed to be strengthened and extra vigilance to be employed along the border from Carlisle in the west to Berwick in the east under the command of his nephew and present heir, John, earl of Lincoln, whom Richard had appointed to his own previously held post under his brother, King Edward, as Lord of the North, based at Middleham Castle in Wensleydale.

On an unusually warm 15 September, Mary went into confinement at Westminster to await the birth of the eagerly anticipated heir. Despite the heat the windows were kept firmly closed and covered by rich tapestries to keep out evil spirits and fires burned day and night in the two large fireplaces to ensure a constant supply of hot water.

Mary was attended by her ladies and by four experienced midwives, two standing by during the daytime and two during the hours of darkness. No men were permitted to enter and that included the royal physicians. Giving birth was a strictly female business. Mary's labour began three days later as Richard, in a state of acute anxiety, paced the floor outside the confinement chamber unconsciously twisting the ring on his middle finger as he waited for news. He was not alone. His closest friends attended him, attempting without much success, to cheer him.

'Here, Dickon' Francis Lovell pressed a flagon of ale into Richard's hand. 'Get this down you and do not worry yourself so much '

'Will you be so calm, Frank, when it is your turn to become a father?' interrupted Richard Ratcliffe with a laugh. 'Isn't the lady Bess with child?'

'Aye' Lovell replied with a rueful grin. 'She is three months gone.'

The daylight was fading when after a twelve hour labour, Mary at last gave birth. Outside the chamber sat Richard, who was fighting to stay awake after two nights without sleep when suddenly he was jerked wide awake by the sound of an infant's cry. Leaping to his feet, he raced to the chamber door but was restrained by Catesby and de Assheton blocking the way.

'Please Dickon,' Catesby cried. 'You know that we men cannot enter there' Suddenly calm, Richard nodded and had just resumed his seat when the door to the birthing chamber was opened and Bess, a huge smile lighting up her flushed face, ran to Richard and flung her arms around his neck crying, 'Dear Uncle Richard, you have a beautiful son.'

'A son, I have a son.'

A wide grin slowly spread across Richard's features as the joyous news sank in then turning back to Bess asked.

'The queen, how fares the queen? '

'Her grace is well. Tired, but very well indeed.'

'Praise be to god '

Richard crossed himself before making his way back to the birth chamber where this time, no one attempted to stop him. He entered quietly and was met by the sight of Mary sitting propped up in bed holding her sleeping baby.

'Here is your son, my dear husband.'

She murmured, holding out the precious tightly swaddled bundle to take into his arms. Richard felt tears of joy pricking his eyelids as he gazed into the face of his son for the first time.

Suddenly, the baby gave a sneeze and opened his eyes and looked upon his father for a moment before going back to sleep.

'Oh, Marie, he is beautiful. Just like his mother.'

Richard reluctantly handed over his son to a waiting nursemaid before bending over his wife and gently kissing her forehead.

'Thank you, my love,' he said quietly, 'Sleep now and we will talk anon.'

Later, when he had retired to bed and was alone with only Rex and Wee Hamish who were now inseparable, for company, Richard gave way to the tears that had threatened all day. Tears of joy mingled with tears of sadness as memories of his first wife, Anne Neville and their son, Edward, flooded back.

The following day the proud new parents discussed the choice of name for the baby prince and finally decided on James, much to the shocked amazement of the nobles and the downright disapproval of Richard's Mother, Cecily.

'What are you thinking of, Richard? ' She demanded. 'How can you even consider giving your son and heir of all things a name favoured by the Scottish Kings?'

'You forget, Ma Mere. My son is half Scottish and his chief godfather will be the young Prince James, duke of Rothesey, and heir to the throne of Scotland *and* first cousin to our son.'

'But, Richard—'

'No buts, Madame'' Richard held up his hand to silence the duchess. 'The matter is not open to discussion.'

Cecily stared into her son's implacable eyes and knew that he would not be moved. Sweeping him a deep curtsey, she quitted the chamber.

Richard and Mary had thought long and hard about the choice of name. Mary had first suggested Richard but the king demurred, saying that his name was not always a wise choice, at the same time ruling out Edward because it revived painful memories of his beloved late son who also had borne that name. Recalling that the baby bore a strong resemblance to Mary, Richard made the momentous decision that James would be their son's name, much to Mary's delight.

The little prince's baptism took place five days later in St Stephen's Chapel within the Palace of Westminster. The sacred ceremony began with Bess, as godmother, proudly carrying the sleeping prince dressed in a christening robe of white satin, beautifully embroidered with sunnes and roses, to the font. Her husband, Francis Lovell, walked beside her, who in the absence of the godfather, James, Duke of Rothesy, stood as proxy.

The only member of the family not present at the baptism was Mary, who following custom, had to yet undergo the ceremony of churching which marked her departure from confinement and her return to public life.

# 20

The next two years passed relatively peacefully giving Richard the opportunity to implement certain changes in the laws of the land. One of his most welcome actions saw the end of the hated act known as ' Benevolences ' which was originally introduced during the reign of his brother, Edward IV, in an effort to raise money for his war against France in 1475, a tax that didn't appear to be a tax but fooled no one.

The Christmas of 1487 was the reason for a double celebration. For not only was the birth of the Christ child celebrated but also the birth on Christmas Eve of a healthy second son for Richard and Mary who this time *was* named Richard, which secretly pleased his proud father.

1488 dawned calmly without a hint of the dramatic events that would shortly unfold north of the border in Scotland. The first hint of impending trouble came from Richard's nephew, John, earl of Lincoln, who in his capacity of his uncle's representative in the north had been keeping a close watch on events from the English side of the border lands. The news that filtered through was disturbing, especially for Mary who confided her fears to Richard.

'I am so concerned, Richard. I fear that my foolish brother has antagonised parliament by creating his second son Duke of Ross and who has always been his favourite. Not only that, but he has also promoted four low born laird's to full lords of parliament without the parliament's approval. This stupid act can only end in disaster,' she cried, wringing her hands. Richard took her into his arms, comforting her with calming words.

'We can only stand by and wait to see what happens next,' he said quietly. 'Does your brother truly prefer his younger son to his first born?' Richard asked.

'Och aye,' Mary answered shaking her head.

'He has never made any secret of it right from the word go, and even named him James too.'

'What about his third son. Is he a James also? '

'Nay, he is named John, a lovely wee lad.'

Despite the severity of the winter weather that lingered in the north. Mary received a missive delivered by an exhausted Scottish messenger, shivering with cold on a raw morning on the third of March. To her surprise, the missive bore the seal of her eldest nephew, James, duke of Rothesay. With trembling hands, Mary broke the seal and quickly read.

*Right trusty and well beloved aunt, god give you greetings, This day with the help of the noble Lords Home and Bothwell, I have escaped the clutches and evil intent of my lord father, who would keep me confined, or worse. Dearest aunt, I greatly fear that civil war with all its evils has come to our beloved Scotland once again. Brought about by the foolishness of my lord father, the king who only listens to the evil counsels of his favourites who would deprive me of my future inheritance of the throne in favour of my younger brother, and heeds not those nobles who would serve him well. Written this second day of February in the year of our lord 1488 at Stirling by your grace's nephew, James, duke of Rothesay.*

Mary hastened to Richard with the disturbing news and found him dictating a letter to his secretary, John Kendall. Both men looked up in alarm when Mary burst in upon them, waving the missive in the air.

'Forgive me, husband for my intrusion, but my business is urgent'

'Pray leave us, Kendall. We will resume our business later''

Kendall rose and bowed to the King and Queen then hastily gathered a bundle of documents and left the chamber, quietly closing the door behind him.

'Do you bring news from Scotland, Marie? '

Richard strode to her side and guided her to his vacated chair before taking the missive from her and quickly scanning the contents.

'Phew!' He exclaimed, letting out a deep breath then glancing at his wife.

'You Scots certainly do not let the grass grow beneath your feet. Do you really think that your nephew is in danger from his father?'

'I think that he is in more danger from the likes of the earls of Argyll and Angus who are well aware that young as he is, James would not be a malleable king like his father but his own man'

Richard nodded and began twisting the ring on his little finger as was his custom when he was in deep thought. He spoke again at length.

'I cannot intervene directly in Scottish matters but I will direct my nephew, Lincoln, to receive prince James and to secure his safety if he is ever forced to flee into England. This is all that we can do at present.'

'Thank you, Richard. I only hope and pray that that never happens.'

# 21

In late Spring Richard decided that the court would move north for the summer to his old home at Middleham . Ever since the death of his wife, Anne, Richard had avoided the castle in the Yorkshire dales, knowing that he would be overwhelmed by memories of their happy past life there. But, he knew that the time had now come to move on and to introduce his present wife and children to the place he had always regarded as home.

Richard wasn't the only person to look forward to returning to Yorkshire. Tom Murgatroyd could not contain his excitement at the thought of going back to the small town of his birth.

'Is Middleham a bonny place then, Tom?' laughed Jeanie McColl, highly amused by Tom's exuberance.

'Bonny? Bonny doesn't even begin to describe it, lass,' enthused Tom. 'A man can breathe in the reet good fresh air theer and walk for miles in't wide open spaces with only the curlews and the sheep for company.'

'I take it that you won't be sorry to leave London then?'

'Leave London, leave London. I tell you, I wouldn't give a flying fart if I never set foot in this stinkhole ever again'

'Oh, Tom,' Jeanie giggled. 'You have such a way with words.'

It was with mixed feelings that Richard led the cavalcade up the main street of Middleham towards the Castle with Mary riding beside him. To his relief, the townspeople had turned out in large numbers and greeted him with cheers and whistles and cries of, 'Welcome home, your grace.'

Richard halted the procession in the market square and signalled to all the mounted company, including himself and Mary, to dismount to receive a blessing from the clergy of the Parish Church of St Alkelda where he had founded a college here in Middleham and also another at Barnard Castle in Co Durham.

Before remounting, the royal couple received a loyal address from the Mayor with a special message of welcome for their new Queen on her first visit to Middleham to which she graciously replied amid cheers. Once more mounted on their horses, they continued up the main street until Mary caught sight of Middleham's magnificent castle towering above the town's much smaller buildings to her left before, led by Richard, she turned and clattered over the drawbridge and into the inner bailey. Looking around her as she dismounted, she turned to Richard saying.

'This castle is truly wonderful, Richard. I look forward to getting further acquainted with it.'

'And I look forward to being your guide, Marie,' he replied with a smile.

The date of their arrival at Middleham was the eleventh of June 1488 but that date was not yet of significance to Richard and Mary as they settled themselves down for the night after their journey with Richard dismissing Tom with,

'Be off and visit your family now, Tom, I can manage without you for the next two or three days.'

'Thank thee kindly, your grace. I shall be reet glad to see 'ow me brother is doing down int old 'ouse.'


Summer that year came early to the Dales so Richard took advantage of the glorious weather to show Mary the beautiful countryside that surrounded Middleham. She was especially impressed by the spectacular Aysgarth Falls whose rushing waters reminded her of similar falls in the Highlands. But most of all, she was deeply touched by the warm welcome that she received from the local people, for, as she confided to Richard,

'I am a stranger to these parts, *and* a Scot to boot. I have been most pleasantly surprised '

'But that is how northern folk are,' explained Richard with a laugh. 'They are excellent judges of character and recognise a genuinely good person when they see one. And by the same token, you wouldn't have been left in any doubt if they *had* taken a dislike to you '

Richard also took Mary on a tour of the great castle and she listened intently as he showed her every nook and cranny and told her about his youth, learning about the art of warfare and the laws of chivalry from his cousin, the earl of Warwick, 'The kingmaker' along with Francis Lovell, Rob Percy, Richard Ratcliffe, etc, and all the other friends he made in those far off days.

He also told her how he grew to love his little cousin, Anne, Warwick's youngest daughter and of their separation when he was forced to give his loyalty to either Warwick or to his brother, king Edward, when those two most powerful men in the kingdom became enemies.

'There was never any question of who I would choose,' he continued. 'Edward was my brother *and* my King.' He shrugged. 'It was many years before I came back here to Middleham. By then Warwick was dead, killed fighting against my brother, and I, at last, was wed to my Anne.'

A faraway look came into Richard's eyes as he recalled the past. 'We returned here to Middleham and made it our home. We were so happy here. Our son, Edward, was actually born in this very chamber. I am so glad that I decided to return.' He turned towards Mary smiling. 'I can almost smell Anne's perfume. I feel that she is still here and that she will walk through that door at any moment.'

Sudden tears welled up in Mary's eyes and threatened to spill down her cheeks as she listened. Realising that while Richard was unfailingly kind and loving towards her, she would never replace Anne Neville in his heart.

Richard halted in mid speech as he noticed Mary's tears.

'Why, Marie, have I said something to distress you?' he asked, putting his arm around her. 'I did not mean to upset you. If I did, please forgive me.'

Mary smiled up at him, wiping her eyes with a kerchief. 'No, Richard. I am just being foolish but I found your story very moving.'

'I have talked enough,' he said, patting her shoulder. 'Come, let us go outdoors and see which noisy game the children are playing.'

# 22

On the thirtieth of June as Richard and Mary were eating dinner seated at the high table in the Great Hall, a messenger wearing the badge of Richard's nephew, John, earl of Lincoln, who was presently in residence at Berwick castle, entered the hall and strode up to the dais and fell to his knees before the king and Queen. The onlookers and the musicians playing in the gallery fell silent as the messenger in his travel stained clothing, produced a sealed parchment and held it up to hand to Richard who asked in his usual calm voice.

'You bring news from my nephew? '

'Aye, your grace. My lord of Lincoln has sensational news from Scotland.'

'What is this this so called sensational news then?'

The messenger glanced uneasily at Mary whose face had turned white with her hand held over her mouth.

'Perhaps, under the circumstances, I should impart the news to your grace alone.'

Richard glanced at Mary, nodded and started to rise to his feet.

'I will join you if I May, my lord.'

'Of course you may, my lady'

Offering her his hand and ignoring the hastily rising company, Richard led the way to their private chamber where he quietly instructed Tom to bring Jeanie to stand outside the door.

'For the Queen may soon have need of her'

'I'll see to it reet away, your grace,' Tom whispered closing the door quietly behind him.

Once seated, Richard commanded the messenger to begin.

'Your graces,' he coughed and cleared his throat before continuing. 'Your pardon, your graces. On the eleventh day of this month at Sauchieburn, near Stirling, the forces of the king of Scots engaged in battle with the forces in support of the Duke of Rothesey.

During or slightly after which, king James was slain and the Duke of Rothesey was immediately proclaimed as King James IV.'

'What do you mean by slain either in battle or slightly afterwards?' Mary interrupted harshly. 'Was my brother killed honourably in battle or not?'

The messenger knelt twisting his hat awkwardly in his hands.

'We do not know for sure, your grace. But rumours abound that his grace was killed while fleeing the field. I deeply regret being the bearer of such distressing news to your grace.'

'Thank you. You may leave us now,' Richard dismissed him with a wave of his hand.

'Your pardon, your grace, but there is more.'

'Then continue '

The messenger again cleared his throat.

'The new monarch was crowned as King James IV at Scone on the twenty fourth day of this month and his late father has been interred at Cambuskenneth Abbey beside his wife, the late Queen Margaret.'

Once more standing upright, the messenger bowed before hastily quitting the chamber.

'So, my foolish brother is dead and my fifteen year old nephew is now king.'

Richard stared at Mary in surprise as he listened to her clipped, cold tones, the likes of which he had never heard her use before.

'I do not deny that James was not the wisest of rulers but he did not deserve to be murdered.'

'We have no proof that he *was* murdered,' countered Richard. 'In time the truth will no doubt out.'

'Knowing my nephew, James would never have countenanced the murder of his father.'

'He is but a lad of only fifteen years and he may have been overruled.'

'Never!' retorted Mary. 'If my brother *was* murdered, it would have been without James' knowledge.'

Seeing that it was pointless to pursue the matter any further as Mary was clearly in a state of shock, he pressed her shoulder in unspoken sympathy and signalled to the hovering Jeanie to attend her mistress, he left the chamber.

# 23

Six weeks had passed and it was on a beautiful day in mid-August when Richard and Mary set off on their journey north to Berwick. The moors surrounding Middleham were ablaze with purple heather and the sound of birdsong filled the air. Richard let out a deep sigh of pure pleasure as he rode alongside Mary, so close together that their horses were almost touching.

'Ah, A day like this makes one feel glad to be alive ' He mused.

'Aye, we don't get blessed with many days like this'

Mary agreed with a smile, watching as Rex and Wee Hamish bounded ahead, only stopping to cock their legs up against a handy bush.

In the weeks following the crowning of Scotland's new young king, the lines of communication between the neighbouring realms had been very busy with couriers riding back and forth with news and messages. The outcome of all this activity was a meeting being arranged between both kings near Berwick, right on the border of both kingdoms.

On the arrival of Richard and Mary with their large retinue at Berwick, the weather had changed. In place of the sun that had shone for them all the way from Middleham, dark clouds scurried across the sky, blown ashore by the strong winds and rain that buffeted the North Sea coast from Berwick all the way south as far as Scarborough.

Huddled in heavy cloaks against the unseasonal weather, the weary travellers thankfully rode across the drawbridge and into the castle that brooded over the town of Berwick and the surrounding Borderlands, the River Tweed and out to the sea. The entire garrison was drawn up to greet them led by the Earl of Lincoln, who dropped to his knees despite the rain to welcome the king and the Queen. 'God's greetings to you my lord uncle and my lady aunt.'

He cried, first kissing Richard's hand and then Mary's. 'Welcome to Berwick. Pray enter. Indoors you will find that fires and hot food await you.'

A change into dry clothing and a hot meal later. Richard and Mary, together with their fellow travellers, were soon feeling much more relaxed as they sat at their ease with their host before a roaring fire.

'A great fire such as this should not be needed at this time of the year,' mused Richard, twirling a goblet of fine red wine around in his hand.

'You forget, Richard,' Mary commented. 'That Scotland can be somewhat chilly, even in summertime.'

'But *you* also forget that we are not in Scotland, wife, but in the northernmost tip of England,' Richard reminded her coldly. 'Berwick has been possessed by England since my victory of 1482.'

Mary looked crestfallen. 'Forgive me. Richard. I meant no offence.'

Richard immediately felt contrite as he looked into Mary's woebegone face. 'I am so sorry, Marie, if I have upset you. It is just that Berwick is a sensitive point with me.'

'As it is with us Scots.'

After an awkward moment's silence. Mary rose and patted his hand. 'Come, let us to bed and no more arguments eh!'

Richard downed the wine in gulp and smiling ruefully, followed his wife to their chamber.


The next day dawned promising to be fair with the last of the wind and rain blown away during the night. Just before noon a Scottish herald arrived and announced that king James and his entourage had set up camp at nearby Lamberton Kirk, situated right on the border between the two kingdoms, and that his King eagerly awaited to greet his fellow sovereign and his dear aunt at their graces convenience. Richard bade the herald to inform King James that he and Queen Mary also anticipated the meeting and that they would gladly wait upon their royal nephew at the hour of two of the clock this afternoon.

At precisely two o'clock, the English visitors arrived outside Lamberton kirk to a fanfare of trumpets. They were accompanied by Mary's two eldest children and the Earls of Lincoln and Northumberland, the Duke of Norfolk and by Francis Lovell, Rob Percy and Richard Ratcliffe and by their various attendant s plus fifty men at arms.

An elaborate canvas pavilion colourfully embroidered with the arms of Scotland glinting in the sunshine, stood beside Lamberton's kirk. Directly in front of which stood young king James of Scotland, the fourth of that name. He was attended by the Earls of Angus and of Argyll and the heads of the Hepburn and Home families. Richard and Mary dismounted from their horses and began to walk forward to be met by James who with a huge smile lighting up his face, had also advanced to meet his guests.

'Welcome, welcome to Scotland, your grace of England and a special welcome back to my dear aunt, more beautiful than ever.'

Mary gazed up at him in amazement as he bent to kiss her hand and cheek, at how tall and handsome her nephew had grown with his shoulder length auburn hair, sparkling eyes and wide shoulders which made him look much older than his fifteen years. Turning to Richard, James held out his hand to greet his fellow sovereign saying.

'God's greeting to your grace' Adding with a wink, 'Or may I address you as my lord uncle? '

'You may gladly call me uncle, nephew.'

Trying not to laugh, Richard took the young King's hand and shook it vigorously.

'Come, let us away inside where refreshments await us,' James pointed to the pavilion entrance and with a bow, offered his arm to Mary.

Once inside he led the way to a small curtained off section, waving the following lords towards the larger section where a long table laden with a wide variety of food, fine wines and ale awaited the English nobles and their Scottish counterparts.

Once alone with Richard and Mary, the smile faded from James' face and he suddenly looked young and vulnerable as he sank down onto a stool saying softly.

'I expect that you are both aware of what befell my lord father after the battle? '

'We have heard various accounts of what happened following Saucieburn,' Richard answered, taking a seat opposite James.

'All I know is that the king, my father, was done to death supposedly fleeing the field.'

James eyes searched both their faces before continuing in a low but clear voice, 'I swear by all that is holy that I never condoned that murder. Indeed, I knew nothing about it until I was informed that I was now king.'

With tears rolling down his cheeks James sobbed, 'I wanted you to know that, aunt Mary.'

'Oh, Jamie,' Mary knelt before her distraught nephew and gathered him into her arms rocking him gently. 'I knew that you could never be guilty of such a heinous crime.'

James wiped his eyes with the back of his hand before continuing, 'All the same, I feel responsible that the foul deed was done in my name. I will carry that guilt for the rest of my life.'

Richard pressed a reassuring hand on the young king's shoulder saying, 'I know exactly how you feel, lad, for I was judged by many to have murdered two of my nephews who were in my care until the truth finally emerged.'

'I thank you for understanding, my lord uncle.'

As James rose to his feet he accidently brushed against Mary who felt something heavy around his waist beneath his clothing.

'What are you wearing, Jamie?' she asked curiously. 'It feels like armour.'

'It is a chain of iron,' James replied with an embarrassed shrug. 'I have vowed to wear it until I have avenged my lord father's murder.'

James' mood suddenly changed back to being the smiling host again. 'Where are my cousins, little Robert and Elizabeth, aunt Mary? I swear I will not recognise them now that they will have grown.'

'They are excited at the thought of seeing you too, Jamie,' she smiled. 'I will have them brought in immediately.'


Later, after enjoying an excellent repast, the serious business of the day was conducted between the two kings and their assorted nobles which resulted in a peace and trade treaty being agreed upon by both nations and to strengthen the agreement, a betrothal between King James and Richard's niece, Lady Margaret of Clarence.

The time finally arrived for the farewells to be said as Richard and Mary prepared to mount their horses to return to Berwick. James and Richard warmly shook hands and clasped each other round the shoulder. Then James fondly kissed his aunt and two small cousins and waved goodbye with cries of, 'God speed' as Richard led the English entourage back across the border.

'What did you think of my nephew, Richard?' Asked Mary as they rode.

'He is a grand lad who, god willing, has all the makings of a fine king, maybe even a great one given time.'

Richard glanced at Mary with his warm smile that never failed to melt her heart.

'I felt a great affinity with him. He reminded me of myself at the same age.'

'I could see that he thought the same about you too, my love,' Mary nodded in agreement.

# 24

A few days after the visit to Scotland The court began the long journey south from Berwick stopping en route at Middleham in order to collect the two young princes, James and Richard, before proceeding at a leisurely pace towards London. On their arrival at the Palace of Westminster Both Richard and Lovell where pleasantly surprised to be greeted in private by Richard's niece, Lady Elizabeth. Who dropped a quick curtsey to her uncle before flinging herself into her startled husband's arms.

'Bess .What brings you here? I thought you were still at Minster Lovell?' He cried before kissing her soundly on the lips.

'I have not seen you all summer long and I have missed you dreadfully, Francis.'

'Aye, I have missed you too, my love,' Lovell smiled. 'Has my wife your leave to remain at court, Dickon? '
Lovell asked while gently removing her arms from around his neck.

'Why certainly, Frank ' Richard laughed.

'After all you spend most of your time in attendance on me here than you do at your own home. The Queen will be pleased to have Bess back with us also'

'Oh thank you, uncle Richard' Bess kissed her uncle's cheek and then with his permission, left to renew her acquaintance with Mary in the Queen's solar.

The only other person not pleased to be at Westminster, apart from Richard, whose dislike of both Westminster and the city was well known, was Tom Murgatroyd whose morose expression was commented on by Richard as his body servant helped him to disrobe for the night.

'What ails thee, Tom?' he asked.

'You look more miserable than usual. Have you been having words with Jeanie again?'

'Nay, sire 'Tom sniffed. 'It's just the thought of being stuck back here in this stinkhole of a town for the coming winter'.

'It doesn't stink quite as badly in the winter,' Richard hid a smile. 'Never mind, Tom, you still have Jeanie to cheer you up'

The close friendship between the two royal servants had blossomed after a shaky start much to the secret amusement of those closest to the King and the Queen and some had even placed bets on when the pair would finally wed.

'Jeanie is a good lass and she doesn't like it much 'ere either, Sire'

'Don't worry, Tom, the Queen and I have decided to spend the coming Christmas season at Windsor.'

This news produced a ghost of a smile on Tom's face.

'Eh, Sire, that castle is a reet gradely place, but not as gradely as Middleham.'

'I am glad that our decision meets with your approval, Tom. I bid you goodnight.'

Clicking his fingers to Rex and Wee Hamish to follow him and grinning to himself, Richard entered his bed chamber closing the door behind him.

Mary was delighted to welcome Bess back with her again. They had so much to talk about. Bess began by offering Mary her condolences on the death of her brother in such horrific circumstances.

'Thank you, my dear. I know that you would understand because you know what it is to lose not one, but two brothers in a similar way.'

Tears filled Bess' eyes as she recalled having to give her mother, the former Queen Elizabeth, the news that her sons had been done to death in the Tower not at Richard's command, whom Elizabeth was convinced was guilty of the murders of his nephews, but at the connivance of Margaret Beaufort, her husband, Lord Thomas Stanley, and that unholy bishop, John Morton. And her mother's unrestrained fury when she realised that she had been duped by the very people that she had plotted with in an attempt to make Bess Queen by marrying her to Margaret Beaufort's son, Henry Tudor after he had successfully invaded the country and made himself king. But that was not to be and instead of being honoured as Queen

Dowager, Elizabeth Woodville, now known as Dame Grey, from her first marriage, had chosen to live in virtual seclusion across the Thames in Bermondsey Abbey where her reluctant daughters visited her from time to time.

Between the return to Westminster and the court's departure to celebrate the Christmas Festival at Windsor Richard was busily occupied attending daily to the affairs of state. He had also made meticulous plans for the constructing of a large chantry at York Minster which he intended to be the eventual final resting place of himself and his descendants. He kept a close watch on the building progress by receiving regular written reports from both the Architect and the Master Builder.

He now also had the opportunity to implement certain acts of parliament that he did not have the time to introduce before Bosworth, namely, the introduction of trial by jury in which the accused was innocent until proven guilty.

Also the bail system which protected suspected offenders from being imprisoned prior to their trial. Richard was well aware that the whole legal system was open to abuse of all kinds and was determined to stamp it out. He also made it illegal to seize a person's property until that person was convicted. He also ensured that only men of good character and owners of property could serve on a jury.

Two acts that won him the approval of his ordinary working people were that the statutes regarding the laws of the land were to be translated from Latin and French into English so all could understand them. The other act instigated by Richard was known as the 'Court of Requests' an early form of legal aid which ensured that the poor had access to legal representation.

However, Richard's most popular act by far was the abolition of the hated 'Benevolences' that had been introduced by his brother, Edward IV to finance his war with France which was a demand for money that had not been sanctioned by parliament and was therefore illegal.

A modest man in many ways, Richard was deeply moved by the cheers that greeted him whenever he appeared in public which he always acknowledged with a wave and his quiet smile.

Shortly after their arrival at Windsor, two weeks before Christmas. Mary confided to Richard that she was once more with child.

'This is wonderful news!' He cried, drawing her into an embrace. 'Are you certain, my love?'

'Aye, husband, I am certain all right 'She laughed.

'When do you expect to be confined? '

'Around the middle of June if all goes well '

'What do you mean by that, Marie? ' Richard asked, with an anxious look in his eyes. 'Are you unwell?'

'No. I am fine'' Mary reassured him. 'Although I am a woman in her thirties and this is my third pregnancy in as many years. But you need not worry, Richard, we Scots are made of stern stuff.'


Once the Christmas festivities were well behind them, another event added to the celebrations that welcomed the arrival of the year 1489, when Tom Murgatroyd and Jeanie McColl were at last married in the still uncompleted Royal Chapel of St George at Windsor, and were honoured by the presence of the King and Queen. There was much merriment at the celebratory feast that followed the ceremony with many bawdy jests, not just from their fellow servants but also from the nobles present when the time came to escort the newly married pair to their bedchamber.

Finally, after ushering out the noisy crowd of Well Wishers, Richard, with a wink at the embarrassed bridegroom, closed the chamber door quietly behind him.

# 25

Following a relatively quiet winter, the middle of March 1489 saw Richard riding north to attend a meeting of the Council of the North at Sheriff Hutton. He was accompanied by Richard Ratcliffe, Rob Percy and William Catesby in his capacity as Chancellor of the Exchequer and Speaker of the House of Commons. Francis Lovell did not ride with them at this time as he had begged leave to remain behind at Westminster with his wife, Bess, who in the second month of pregnancy was causing him much concern as she was far from well. Richard also had another more personal reason for returning north.

Back in January 1472, a few months prior to his marriage to Anne Neville on the 12th July of that year. Richard had a brief affair with a young gentlewoman in the household of his mother, Duchess Cecily. The outcome of which resulted in the birth of a son and the death of the young mother. By this time Richard and Anne were living at Middleham in far off Wensleydale so Cecily sent a messenger to inform Richard that he was now the father of a motherless son. Full of remorse for his past brief fling and for the death of the young woman, he begged his mother to make arrangements for the care of his son whom Cecily had, without informing him, named Richard. The child was eventually placed in the care of a local Schoolmaster and his wife whose own baby had recently died at birth. At his home in the North, Richard was kept fully informed of the events by his mother and made arrangements for a yearly payment to be made towards the child's upkeep. The person Richard assigned to deliver the payments was Francis Lovell whom he knew could be trusted implicitly with such a delicate mission.

The boy grew up fully aware that while he had taken their name, Master and Mistress Broom, the schoolmaster and his wife were not his real parents but that didn't prevent him from enjoying a happy childhood in which he developed a love of scholarly books inspired by his schoolmaster guardian. Although Richard received regular reports on the boy's progress over the years, he had never actually met him until just before he left London for the last time prior to the battle of Bosworth. He decided that the time was now right to make himself known to his son so he sent Lovell to bring the boy to him at Baynards Castle, his mother's London home on the banks of the Thames in the city where they could meet well away from the curious stares of the courtiers at Westminster.

Richard would never forget the first time that he laid eyes on his thirteen year old son who bore his name. The youth was nothing like his father Richard in appearance, having a mass of pale blond hair and being of stocky build. The boy had looked about him, nervously shuffling his feet as he entered the sumptuously furnished chamber urged on by Lovell who had escorted him here from his home in the city. He then noticed the richly dressed man clad in black and purple velvet with a glittering golden chain made up of sunnes and roses across his shoulders approaching him with a reassuring smile and asking him in a warm low voice.

'Do you know who I am, Richard?'

'No, no, Sir ' He stammered, looking wildly around. 'Sorry, Sir, but I do not know who you are '

The man now stood in front of him and placing a hand on his trembling shoulder told him, 'I am your father, lad, and also your king. Come and sit with me and I will explain.'

Dumbfounded with shock and unable to speak, young Richard quietly followed and listened while his newly found father explained to him the circumstances surrounding his birth, ending with the promise that, 'If I defeat the Tudor in the coming battle, I will acknowledge you as my son and you will take your place here at court. But if I am defeated, you must tell no one who you are for your own safety. Do you understand, my son?'

Young Richard nodded, trying to absorb such amazing news. After a few moments he said shyly. 'My adopted father, Master Broom, Is moving to a new school near to Ashford in Kent where I have the opportunity to be apprenticed to a Master Stone Mason.'

'And is it your wish to become a Master Stone Mason one day? '

The boy's face lit up as he answered eagerly. 'Oh yes, my lord. I want nothing more than to be a master of that trade when I am fully grown'

'Then that is what you must become.' Richard heaved a secret sigh of relief that he would not need to introduce his bastard son publicly.

'You must let me keep track of your progress, lad, and we must sometimes meet again '

'I would like that very much. I thank you, my lord,' Young Richard replied shyly.


Richard recalled that meeting as on a breezy, but fine morning he rode into the precincts surrounding York Minster to inspect the progress on the building of his family Chantry. The deafening sounds of hammering and of men hauling large slabs of stone up on pulleys by the scaffolding met him as he dismounted and handed his reins to a hovering groom. Waiting to greet him were the Dean and the Master Mason bowing obsequiously as Richard, followed by Richard Ratcliffe, entered the partially constructed Chantry. It promised to be the handsome building that Richard had envisaged when he had first commissioned its construction. He nodded his satisfaction as the Master Mason drew his attention to the ceiling with its elaborately carved Angels and Yorkist Roses that had just recently been completed. But all the time that the Master Mason was explaining how the work had progressed, Richard's eyes were searching the faces of the young apprentices as they carried out their allotted tasks until at last, he glimpsed his son. He knew that he was apprenticed to this particular Master Mason, and it was for this reason that he had been granted the contract for the construction of the King's Chantry.

The tour over, Richard thanked the Master Mason and informed the Dean that he would now take refreshment in his office across the yard and that one of the apprentices could wait upon him.

'That one looks capable.'

He said casually pointing to his son. 'It shall be done at once, your grace.'

The Dean bowed and led the way outside. Once inside the office, Richard dismissed the surprised Dean with a wave of his hand saying.

'You must have many duties to attend to. You have our leave to depart.'

As the apprentice hesitated at the door bearing a tray loaded with cakes, ale and wine, Richard signalled him forward. 'Enter, lad.'

Then turning to a startled Ratcliffe, asked him to stand outside and not to allow anyone to enter.

'Are you sure, Sire? ' Ratcliffe asked with a worried frown.

'I am sure, Dick. Don't worry, I shall explain later. Meanwhile remember, no one is to enter.'

Closing the door firmly behind him, Richard turned and faced his son. Striding up to him, he clasped both arms onto his shoulders thus preventing him from kneeling and oblivious to the dust that arose from the young man's work clothes.

'How are you, lad?'

'I am well, your grace.'

The voice that answered Richard was no longer the voice of the child that he remembered but that of a man. In the four years since they had first met. Richard Broom was now a strapping young man of seventeen. As tall as his father but much more broadly built. He had the same shock of unruly blond hair but there the resemblance to the child that he had been ended.

Richard shook the stone dust from his hands and indicating a chair, bade his son to be seated.

'Are you happy in your apprenticeship?' he asked, taking a seat opposite him.

'Oh aye, my lord,' His son answered with a smile that lit up his whole face.

'I couldn't imagine following any other trade '

'Son, that makes me very happy ' said Richard.

'Is your home still in Kent? '

'Yes, Sire. My father has just recently purchased a—' he broke off abruptly as he realised that he had unthinkingly referred to Master Broom as 'Father'.

'Carry on, Richard, Master Broom has been much more of a father to you than I have ever been, alas,' smiled Richard ruefully.

'I am so sorry, Sire,' Flushing painfully. 'As I was saying, Master Broom has purchased a dwelling on the Eastwell estate near to Ashford '

'Is that a pleasant place to live? I am not very familiar with Kent.'

'Oh yes, Sire. It is very pleasant indeed. I would be happy to retire there with my books when I am an old man.'

'That is a long time in the future,' Laughed Richard. 'Meanwhile, Son, knowing your love of books, I have brought you a small gift that I hope you will enjoy.'

Reaching into the leather pouch that hung from his belt, Richard handed him a small book beautifully tooled in Red leather with the title 'The Canterbury Tales by Geoffrey Chaucer ' engraved in gold letters.

'I cannot thank you enough, your grace. It is wonderful.' Whispered young Richard, awestricken.

'Look inside, I have written something on the flyleaf for you.'

Almost reverently he opened the book and when he saw what his father had written there, tears filled his eyes as he read in Richard's firm hand.

*'To my dear son. I hope that you will remember me whenever you open this book. Your loving father, R.'*

'Sire, I shall treasure this forever and I shall never forget you or this day. Thank you,' he murmured kneeling and kissing his father's hand. Brushing away the tears that threatened to spill down over his cheeks, young Richard arose and fumbling inside the pocket of his work smock, produced a small angel carved from clear white marble and shyly offered it to Richard.

'Would you care to have this, my lord? I am sorry that it is not very good.'

'But it is exquisite.' Richard carefully took the small Angel, examining it closely. 'I thank you, Richard. You are a true artist, and I too will treasure this gift.'

Father and son smiled at each other as Richard placed the little carved Angel carefully into his pouch, and rising from his chair moved slowly towards the door saying.

'I regret that this meeting has had to be such a short one, lad, but I am so glad to know that you have a happy life '

His son also rose to his feet and bowing low replied, 'I thank you, my lord, for today. I shall never forget it.'

'Nor will I, Richard Broom.'

The King suddenly let out a loud laugh and with one hand on the door handle remarked, 'You realise of course, son, that you DO bear my full name don't you?'

'Aye, Sire. I know that Planta Genista, Plantagenet, is the Latin for a Sprig of Broom.'

# 26

Richard returned south a month later, his business in the north complete after brief visits to Middleham and to his fortresses at Penrith and Barnard Castle where he found everything in order. Despite his dislike of London, he was glad to be back and surrounded by his extended family once more who gave him a great welcome as he dismounted from White Surrey and hurried up the steps to where they greeted him led by Mary whose healthy looks belied her seven months of pregnancy.

'Why, my love, you are positively glowing,' he exclaimed, managing to take her into his arms and kiss her soundly despite her bulk. He suddenly felt a sharp tugging on the edge of his cloak followed by a little voice calling plaintively.' I am here too, papa ' ' And so you are, little man ' Richard stooped and swept his eldest son, James up with one arm and took his younger brother, Richard, from his nurse with his other as surrounded by other family members including Mary 's two children and the wildly excitedly barking Rex and Wee Hamish, he led the way into the palace.

Later, during a quiet moment while he sat at his desk scanning various documents presented to him by Secretary John Kendall, he was approached by Francis Lovell.

'May I please beg a word with your grace? ' He asked bowing with the utmost formality while giving a sideways glance and slight nod of the head in the direction of Secretary Kendall.

His meaning was not lost on Richard who dismissed Kendall with 'That will be all for tonight, John.'

Kendall shuffled some papers, bowed and left the two friends alone.

'Did you manage to meet your lad, Dickon?' Lovell immediately dropped the formality once Kendall had left the chamber and flopped down onto a stool.

'Yes, Frank I did and he is a very talented young man.' Richard passed the small Angel that adorned his desk over to Lovell who let out a low whistle of amazement.

'Phew! Dickon. Did the lad actually carve this?'

'He did,' Richard nodded and continued. 'Despite his gift, he is a very modest young man and has no wish to be acknowledged or to live at court but prefers a quiet life with his books and being able to follow his trade.'

'A wise lad also,' Lovell chuckled.

'Probably,' grinned Richard in agreement then suddenly serious asked. 'Where is Bess, Frank? I expected her to here with you.'

'Bess is not at all well, Dickon, and is resting in bed. She asked me to give you her apologies for not being here welcome you back'

'What ails her? Is it serious?' asked Richard with a worried frown. He was very fond of his niece and didn't wish her to suffer in any way.

'As you are aware, Dickon, Bess is now three months gone with child and is having a really miserable time being constantly sick and with badly swollen ankles.'

'Perhaps she will improve before too long,' mused Richard thoughtfully.' I have heard it said that many pregnant women suffer thus in the first few months.'

'I hope so, Dickon. I hate to see her suffer'.


Richard's prophesy proved to be the correct one and by the time that Mary went into confinement on the 15th June, Bess was feeling much better and no longer suffering constant sickness.

Four days later on June 20th following a particularly difficult labour that lasted over twelve hours, an exhausted Mary finally gave birth to a tiny but perfectly formed baby daughter. The first time that Richard saw his little girl he was totally captivated when the baby grasped his finger in her tiny hand as he looked into her blue - grey eyes so like his own.

'She is beautiful,' he murmured, bending over and gently kissing Mary's forehead.

'I am so sorry that I have failed to give you another son, Richard,' she whispered softly.

'There is nothing to be sorry for, my love. You have given me a perfect daughter for which I truly thank you. rest now and we will talk some more later ' Mary's eyes closed as much needed sleep overcame her and with one last glance at both his wife and his new daughter, Richard almost tip toed from the chamber much to the shocked and horrified midwife and the other ladies present because the king had broken the firmly held rule that disallowed the presence of any male in the confinement chamber but, as Tom Murgatroyd, in his usual characteristic style put it: 'His grace does not give a flying fart for their rules.'

When it came to a choice of name for the baby princess, Richard's first thought was that she be known as Mary. 'Because she is so lovely, just like her mother.'

'You flatter me, dearest. But would you not prefer to call her Anne, in memory of Lady Anne?' She suggested, pressing his hand gently.

Richard looked at his wife in amazement at her generosity. 'Are you sure about that, Marie?'

'I am sure.'

'Then Anne it shall be my dear.'

Francis Lovell became a father for the first time when his wife, Bess gave birth to a healthy son at their home, Minster Lovell, Oxfordshire, exactly three months following the birth of Princess Anne. Richard and Mary sent their congratulations and informed the jubilant Lovell that his son must be baptised in the Royal Chapel of St Stephen's, here in Westminster. To Richard's secret delight, the heir to Lovell's vast wealth, title and estates, was to be named Richard with himself and Mary standing as godparents.

On the day itself, the spectre at the feast was Bess' mother, the former Queen, Elizabeth Woodville, now known as Dame Grey. Everyone who remembered her as King Edward IV's unpopular but beautiful Queen, were shocked by her changed appearance. Gone forever were the dazzling good looks that had captured a king, only to be replaced by a gaunt figure with a lined, wrinkled face who leaned on a cane and dressed in a plain off white woollen gown with a matching wimple covering her greying hair.

Richard greeted her calmly, his impassive face not betraying his dislike of his former sister –in - law as she attempted a curtsey.

'Welcome, Madame.'

'Your grace is...' she purposely hesitated before continuing in an equally cold and distant voice, 'kind.'

Mary had been very curious to meet the former Queen having heard so many tales about Elizabeth's famed beauty coupled with her greed and lust for power.

And as she remarked to Richard when they were alone later, 'It is hard indeed to imagine that lady was once so well known for her beauty.'

'One thing hasn't changed ,though,' Richard spat out tight mouthed. 'She is still a bitch and that will never change.'

Well aware that her husband and his so called sister – in – law had always disliked each other intensely, Mary wisely changed the subject.

# 27

Three years had flown past. Three years in which peace had managed to prevail despite an attempt by the French to seize control of the English enclave of Calais that Richard quickly dispelled in one short but decisive battle that left the French suing for peace.

There was no indication that 1492 would prove to be a momentous year with far reaching consequences for Richard and for the throne as he enjoyed a break from affairs of state with his wife and children around him. He had grown especially close to his step son, Robert Hamilton, over the seven years since he had first arrived in England as a lively six year old for the marriage of his mother to the King. Now, almost thirteen, he was still lively, raising smiles with his antics and followed around adoringly by his young half siblings, James, Richard and toddler Anne.

Elizabeth Woodville died at Bermondsey Abbey following a short illness on the 8th June. And though he did not attend her funeral, Richard arranged for her to be interred beside his brother in St George's Chapel, Windsor.

'That was very generous of you, Richard,' Mary remarked.

'I did it because Edward loved her and would have wished it,' He shrugged. 'The plain slab will only name her as Elizabeth Wydville, that is the original spelling. And not as Queen.'

It was a searing hot day in July without a cloud in the sky, rare in Wensleydale. where the court was in residence at Middleham. The Master of Henchmen had arranged for a series of horse races to take place on the fields behind the castle.

The participants being the gentlemen of the royal household, townspeople, castle employees, and the young noblemen, including Lord Robert, who were training for future knighthood.

'Please, my lady mother,' Robert hopped up and down with excitement at the thought of the first race that he had been allowed to take part in. 'May I beg a favour from you to wear in the race? '

'Of course you may, Robert. If you will keep still for a moment I will tie my blue silk scarf around your arm,' Mary laughingly replied.

'Calm down, lad and concentrate on the race,' Richard advised with a grin.

'Aye, Sire, I promise that I will do you proud.'

With a courtly bow, Robert mounted his horse held by an groom, turned, and trotted towards the starting post.

Benches and stools had been placed on a slightly rising mound overlooking the race track for the use of Mary and her ladies and for all the excited children and their attendants. Also present and lining the track were the castle servants, allowed time off from their duties and beside them, the townspeople of Middleham eager to cheer on their relatives and friends. There was much laughter and jostling for the best places among them and many good-natured wagers were placed. Silence suddenly fell as the trumpets sounded, heralding the start of the first race of the day which was for the castle workers and was won by a young apprentice blacksmith who blushing furiously accepted his prize of a bag of coins with an awkward bow, from his smiling Queen.

After a short respite, the trumpets sounded the start of the second race, the race for the young knights to be which included Robert who waved to his family as he took his place alongside his friends at the start. Another blast from the trumpets and they were off, hooves thundering as the horses and their young riders galloped down the track. Then, disaster struck, silencing the cheers and whistles of the spectators as one of the horses suddenly stumbled throwing its young rider completely over its head and into the path of the oncoming horses whose riders desperately tried to steer them away from the fallen rider who lay motionless on the ground.

Richard leapt to his feet. 'My god!' he cried horror stricken, 'it is Robert who has fallen!' as he started to run towards the track followed closely by Lovell who tried to restrain him.

'Be careful, Dickon. You could be run down.'

But Richard hurried on as the Master of Henchmen signalled wildly to end the race. Mary sat shaking her head in disbelief, white faced with shock and horror as she watched Richard reach her son and cradle him gently in his arms.

'Is he badly hurt, Dickon?' Lovell asked anxiously as he caught up with Richard.

'He is dead, Frank,' he replied tonelessly, at the same time closing Robert's eyes.

Refusing all offers of help, Richard carried Robert's body into the castle chapel and laying him down before the altar, instructed the hovering priest, 'Do not to leave him alone '

He then went to comfort Mary who had fallen into a deep faint before being carried by her ladies into her bed chamber where Richard found them cluttering anxiously around her.

'Leave us ' He ordered curtly. The ladies curtseyed and silently withdrew leaving only Bess kneeling beside Mary and holding her hand.

'You to. Please, Bess. I will stay with my wife now '

'Yes, uncle '

Bess, one hand on the door handle hesitated before quitting the chamber. 'If there is anything I can do to help, Uncle Richard. I will remain close by '

'Thank you, Bess, but there is nothing else that you can do today'

Bess curtseyed and left the chamber closing the door quietly behind her.

Now that they were alone Richard climbed onto the bed and gathered Mary into his arms as she sobbed her heart out.

'My poor wee boy' She gulped with tears streaming down her cheeks. 'He is too young, much too young to die.'

'I know, I know,' Richard murmured stroking her hair.

'How do *you* know? He was *my* son' she cried.

'Robert was like a son to me. And yes, I *do* know what it is like to lose a young son. You forget that my son and heir, Edward, died here at Middleham'

He shook her unintentionally as distress overwhelmed him and Mary, looking up into his face saw his tear filled eyes and his struggle to contain his grief.

'Forgive me, Richard, my love' She whispered softly.

'Of course you know what it is to lose a dear child and will never forget it. I also know that Robert was like a son to you'

Richard held her close and kissing the top of her head, promised that.

'The Chantry at York Minster is almost complete and our sons shall both lie there together until the time that you and I join them, so they will never be alone '

As the last rays of the summer sun began to fade over the city of York on the fifteenth day of September 1492. A cortege bearing two small white coffins passed slowly through the streets watched by the silent tearful crowds who crossed themselves as it passed by. The only sounds were the muffled beat of a single drum leading the way and the clatter of the funeral cart drawn by six black horses, their nodding heads adorned with the black plumes of mourning and the footsteps of the black clad mourners following the coffins led by the king, firmly holding the hand of the heavily veiled Queen.

The procession halted outside the West door of the Minster to be greeted by the tolling of the great bell and the clergy led by the archbishop. The coffin of Prince Edward, draped with the royal arms of England and with the three feathers of the Prince of Wales, had previously been interred temporarily at Jervaulx Abbey, not far from Middleham, until the chantry at York had been ready to receive it, was borne into the Minster by four former gentlemen of his household while that of Lord Robert Hamilton, adorned by the royal arms of Scotland and of the house of Hamilton was similarly borne.

The day following the solemn Requiem Mass and the internments in the almost complete chantry chapel, Richard and Mary returned to Sheriff Hutton where they were met by a curious Edward of Warwick who innocently asked, 'Are my cousins both together in Heaven now, uncle Richard? '

'Yes, Edward, they are' Replied Richard gently.

'Oh good.'

The young man of seventeen who everyone now knew would never progress mentally beyond the age of seven, clapped his hands excitedly 'They will always be able to play together for ever now '

One month later when the court had journeyed south to a subdued Westminster. The peace was shattered by the arrival of a delegation from Scotland with news that shocked Richard and especially Mary, to the core. News that would change their lives for ever.

# 28

Seated on their thrones under the colourful canopy of state richly embroidered with the arms of England in Westminster's great Hall, and attended by both the lords Spiritual and the lords Temporal of the realm, Richard and Mary listened as the Master of Ceremonies announced the arrival of waiting visitors in a ringing voice.

'Make way, make way, for my lord Bishop Elphinstone, Chancellor of Scotland and my lord the Earl of Argyll and my lords Hepburn, Home and Campbell.'

They glanced at each other with mixed feelings of curiosity and some trepidation as the black clad visitors began to make their slow, dignified progress down the hall towards the thrones, finally reaching the dais, they fell to their knees and to the stunned amazement of the assembled onlookers, Bishop Elphinstone addressed not Richard, but Mary.

'God save your grace. Mary, Queen of Scotland and of the Isles. We, your loyal lords, salute you.'

The silence following this totally earth shattering announcement seemed to last for several minutes but it was actually only seconds before Mary's voice, its Scottish accent more pronounced than usual demanded coldly, 'My lords, pray explain yourselves.'

Bishop Elphinstone looked pleadingly at the Queen as he struggled to ease the rheumatic pain in his knees as he continued to kneel.

'I am Bishop Elphinstone, Chancellor of Scotland— ' he began.

'I am well aware of who you are, my lord, 'Mary interrupted him impatiently. 'Why do you address me as your Queen? '

The earl of Argyll broke in as the bishop still hesitated. 'What my lord bishop is trying to say, your graces,' he nodded in Richard's direction to include him in the news that he began to reveal, 'It is to our great sorrow that we bring you the woeful tidings of the deaths of our beloved sovereign lord, King James IV of blessed memory and also of his two brothers, James, Duke of Ross and Archbishop of St Andrews; and John, Earl of Mar.'

Richard then spoke for the first time, bidding the delegates to rise and to Argyll to continue as Mary sat in dazed silence, as she assimilated the astounding news with both a mixture of shock and of sorrow at the deaths of her beloved nephews and her dawning realisation that she was now not only Queen consort of England but also Queen regnant of Scotland and the Isles and all that it implied.

Argyll, a stocky built, slightly balding man in his mid-forties, continued, 'To our great sorrow, King James passed away at Stirling on the 30$^{th}$ day of September, three days following the deaths of his younger siblings. It was all very sudden. A week previously, King James had invited his brothers to join him for a wee spot of hunting when on the second day, on returning to the castle after a guid days sport, Prince John suddenly developed what appeared to be a bit of a cold that quickly turned into a raging fever, sweating and shivering in turn. The next day Prince James also fell ill with the same symptoms along with his squire of the body, a poor wee laddie of only nine.'

At this point in Argyll's narrative he was interrupted by Richard asking tensely, 'By this time, was King James also showing signs of this fever?'

'Nay, your grace,' Argyll answered. 'But the following day, his grace insisted on visiting his brothers in their chamber, despite the physicians pleading with him to stay away as the fever was probably highly contagious.'

'Aye, that sounds like James. He has been... was... always very impulsive,' Mary interjected before signalling Argyll to continue.

'A few hours later that same evening, puir Prince John died calling piteously for his mother in his delirium and just after midnight, God called Prince James to join his brother in Heaven.'

Argyll stopped to mop his brow and Bishop Elphinstone took up the narrative. 'Your graces. It was as the physicians had feared. King James did indeed succumb to the fever and died three days following his brothers after putting up a valiant fight. All three noble princes have since been interred at Cambuskenneth Abbey beside their parents.'

He paused to draw breath before handing to Mary a sealed document bearing the arms of the Scottish Parliament bowing deeply before continuing. 'Therefore, Madam, I and my companions have been given the great honour by parliament of journeying to England to inform your grace that you are now our sovereign lady and that your realm awaits your coming.'

Richard then spoke. 'The Queen and I both thank you, my lords, but you will appreciate that we need time to absorb this news that you bring us and that we also need to discuss this matter in private.'

He rose to his feet and held out his hand to Mary.

'Meanwhile gentlemen, you will be comfortably housed and your needs taken care of and we will speak to you again anon.'

There was much speculation and whispered comments from the Lords and the commons as Richard and Mary left the hall and retired to their private chambers where Tom and Jeanie were in attendance. One look at Richard's stern countenance froze them in their tracks as they prepared to serve their master and mistress with refreshments.

'You may leave us,' He gestured, pointing to the door. 'You will be summoned when her grace and I have need of you'

Bowing and curtseying, Tom and Jeanie hastily left the chamber and made their way to the Servant's Hall where the news from Scotland had already spread like wildfire.

'Hang on 'Yelled Tom, trying to make himself heard above the din. 'What's all this racket about t'Queen? '

'Haven't you heard, Master Murgatroyd?' A young page asked him. 'We thought that you and your wife would have been the first to know.'

'ells bells, lad, spit it out ' Tom fumed, scratching his head.

'Me a'nt wife have been reet busy in't royal chambers and 'ave heard nowt '

'It's our Queen, Master Murgatroyd ' The page cried excitely. 'She is now the Queen of the Scots in her own right as well as consort of our king Richard '

'God's teeth, 'ow can that be?' Gasped Tom turning to Jeanie who was as stunned as her husband.

'Well,' The page began. 'It seems that the king of Scots and his two brothers have both died, so our Queen is Scotland's Queen as well now.'

Everyone then stared at Jeanie who had let out a loud wail of anguish on hearing the news.

'Och those puir bonny lads. I must awa to her grace.'

'Nay, lass' Tom managed to restrain his wife as she made a sudden run for the door. 'Leave it be. Her grace will send for you when she needs you '

'Aye, maybe you are right, Tom' Jeanie slumped onto a stool with a dejected shudder. 'But those puir lads. Something awful must have happened.'

# 29

Shut away from everyone in their private chamber, Richard and Mary began to discuss the implications of what would now become of their changed lives, as she dried her eyes after giving way momentarily to tears of shock and sorrow.

'No time for tears, husband,' Mary spoke resolutely. 'We have much to talk about.'

'We have indeed, Marie' Richard agreed, laying a reassuring hand on her shoulder as he took a seat beside her.

'Do you know how the Scots will accept an English King? '

'But, Richard' Mary answered with a slight frown. 'You will not be King unless you are granted the Crown Matrimonial, until then you will be my consort as I am yours here in England '

Richard leapt to his feet, knocking over his chair in his haste. 'But I am your husband! ' he cried, 'And an anointed king, so how can that be? '

Mary reached for his hand and tried to calm him with soothing words. 'Richard, my love. It is the law in Scotland. Be sure that I will inform parliament that it is my wish to confer upon you the Crown Matrimonial so we will then be joint sovereigns '

'You mean to tell me that parliament must first approve?' Richard asked, shaking his head in disbelief.

'Aye, Richard, but I see no problem. And have you not realised that whatever happens, our little son James is now heir to both our thrones and god willing, will unite our two kingdoms?'

Richard's serious expression faded to be replaced by one of dawning understanding and delight. 'Oh yes,' he breathed, his eyes shining as he visualised a brilliant future. 'With the help of god, we can build a great nation for our son to inherit and it will be a force in the whole of Europe to reckon with.'

A week later, accompanied by the Scottish lords and by leading members of the king's Privy Council and a thousand halberd men and archers along with the sound of trumpets and of drums, Richard and Mary set off on the long journey from Westminster to Scotland. Mounted on White Surrey and holding six year old Prince James before him with Mary, clad in deep mourning, riding beside him on her favourite mount, Black Laddie. They acknowledged the cheers from the crowds of well-wishers watching their departure. Just behind them and pulled by two large horses, rumbled a cart draped in black velvet and which bore in the centre, the fabled Stone of Scone on which all the kings of Scotland had been crowned until Edward 1 removed it to England in 1296 as a trophy of war and placed it under a specially made Coronation Chair in Westminster Abbey. As a gesture of goodwill to both his wife and to the Scottish nation, Richard had announced that the stone would be returned to Scotland.

For, as he had said to Mary, 'It is only right and fitting that you should be crowned Queen at Scone Abbey, sitting on the stone as your ancestors did before you.'

It was a fine autumn day three weeks later when they finally reached the border at Berwick where they were warmly welcomed by Richard's nephew, John de la Pole, earl of Lincoln, Commander of the garrison at Berwick castle.

On the journey from London they had been joined along the way by various nobles and their attendants so by the time that they had arrived in Berwick their ranks had swollen to over two thousand which made Richard wonder how such a large number would find decent lodgings in the small town. He and Mary would be accommodated in the Castle of course, where they could rest comfortably before Mary's triumphant entry into her kingdom.

The momentous day dawned surprisingly fine for the first week in November with only a gentle breeze blowing in from the sea. Magnificently gowned in blue and white velvet with a matching cloak lined with black fur and with a bejewelled coronet encircling her hennin with its long blue veil, Mary entered into her realm at Lamberton with an equally majestically attired Richard wearing a tabard emblazoned with the Royal Arms of England and of France complete with a golden circlet around his helmet at her side, to be greeted by a fanfare of trumpets and by the Archbishop of Glasgow and members of the Scottish Parliament, one of whom knelt before the sovereigns and read out an address of welcome and who could scarcely be heard above the cheers of the onlookers and the peals of the church bells.

Welcoming crowds lined all the route on the two days that it took them to reach the outskirts of Edinburgh where they stayed overnight at Craigmiller Castle to allow them to rest and to prepare for their entry into Scotland's capitol.

The day did not begin well with a with a cold thick sea haar that rolled in from the Forth and hid the city from view, even obscuring the towers of the castle perched high on its hill. The swirling mist produced an eerie silence, the normal everyday sounds of the busy city muffled by the mist that penetrated all the wynds as well as Edinburgh's main thoroughfare, the Royal Mile. But, as the procession approached the city gates, the haar suddenly began to lift and a pale wintery sun began to break through as Richard and Mary began their slow progress down the Royal Mile as the cannons on the castle ramparts thundered out their welcome, almost drowning out the pipes and drums that led the way followed by the Stone of Scone and the mounted king and Queen. The royal children, in an open litter came next and were cheered loudly by the crowds lining the route. They were followed by the English and the Scottish nobles riding side by side and smiling amiably at each other.

At the rear, in one of the many baggage carts sat Tom and Jeanie, struggling to restrain wee Hamish and Rex who were both barking madly at the unaccustomed roar of the cannons assaulting their ears.

'What do ye think of Edinburgh, Tom?' Jeanie shouted in an effort to make herself heard above the din. 'Is it not a braw city?'

'Aye, but it is still a stink hole, like all other cities.' he yelled back.

'Aye, I'll give ye that, lad,' she laughed.

They were still grinning when the procession ground to a halt outside St Giles Cathedral where the clergy waited on the steps before the great door to greet the sovereign. The bells and the cannons fell silent as Richard and Mary dismounted and knelt, holding hands for the blessing as the massed choirs sang a hymn of welcome before they remounted and continued on their way again.

Soon, the almost completed new Palace of Holyrood and the adjoining ancient abbey came into view. Richard stared at the palace and let out a long low whistle of admiration.

'That is a truly beautiful building. Was it begun by your nephew, Marie?' he asked.

'Yes,' she replied. 'He intended it to be the main royal residence here in Edinburgh rather than the Castle which is not the most comfortable place to live.'

Surrounded by several acres of parkland with Salisbury Crags and the massive bulk of the extinct volcano, Arthur's Seat brooding high above it, the new palace and its surroundings made an impressive picture as the procession clattered through the gates. Richard and Mary entered the palace, Richard glancing around with interest as he noted the modern interior, so different from the Palace of Westminster.

'Do you like what you see?' Mary asked her husband, noting his interest.

'Yes indeed. I am quite impressed,' he replied. 'I did not expect this degree of comfort.'

'We scots are not such barbarians as you thought eh?' laughed Mary. 'Of course, it is still unfinished, but I will complete the work begun by my nephew.'

# 30

The court remained in Edinburgh for a week while preparations went ahead for the coronation at Scone Abbey near Perth. Richard took advantage of the time to go hunting and to familiarise himself with the surrounding countryside. He was also kept fully informed of events in England by William Catesby who now held the posts of Chancellor of the Exchequer and Speaker of the House of Commons, who sent him daily messages via Richard's very efficient courier service.

The weather had turned much colder with an overnight frost and winter was now definitely in the air when the cavalcade finally arrived at Scone Palace, very close to the Abbey and to the Moot Hill where Mary's coronation would take place. Despite the onset of winter, Mary and Richard were both well aware that it was essential that her crowning must not be delayed by the weather. Waiting to greet them were the Chieftains of the Highland Clans and their followers whose colourful dress greatly intrigued the English contingent who had never encountered them before. They were even more intrigued by the unknown language spoken by the Clansmen.

'What is this gibberish?' asked Francis Lovell the following day after one of the highlanders accidently collided with him causing him to spill his ale.

'I believe that it is the Gaelic, Frank,' answered Richard Ratcliffe with a shrug.

'Well,' laughed Lovell, 'I believe that the fellow was apologising to me in his own way. These highlanders seem to have good manners despite their barbarous tongue.'

'Which is more than can be said about you, Frank.'

Neither had heard Richard approach them from behind.

'Must I remind you that we are guests in this country and have been accorded every courtesy since our arrival,' he reminded them tersely.

'I am sorry, Sire. I did not mean to cause offence,' Lovell answered shamefaced.

'I know, Frank,' Richard's voice lost its momentary coldness. 'And Gaelic is not a barbaric tongue here,' he paused and continued with a wry smile, 'but English is.'

To say that the coronation ceremony of Queen Mary surprised the English visitors would be something of an understatement. Because the actual crowning took place outdoors on the top of Moot Hill where the Stone of Scone had originally been sited facing the west door of the abbey. It was a bitterly cold, but thankfully dry morning as William Scheves, the Archbishop of St Andrews, followed his cross bearer and monks from the abbey chanting and swaying their censors which caused the sweet smell of incense to be caught on the breeze, led the procession followed by Richard, wearing his own richly embroidered coronation robes and topped by a golden circlet that gleamed and caught the rays of the pale sun as he escorted his wife to her crowning.

Royally robed in a gown of purple velvet embroidered with gold thread and trimmed with ermine and a long matching train and with her hair worn loose and falling in waves to her waist. Mary made a regal figure as she ascended the hill. On reaching the Stone of Scone, also called the stone of Destiny, which was draped in red velvet, and mounted on a dais, Mary took her seat as cheers erupted from the large numbers of onlookers and Richard took his seat on her left. The sound of trumpets heralded the start of the ceremony which began with a short sermon from Bishop Elphinstone.

He was immediately followed by the archbishop of Glasgow laying his hands upon the Queen's head and intoning a blessing before the Ollgmh Righ or Royal Poet, stepped forward and addressed Mary in ringing tones.

'Beonnachd De Righ Alban.'

Or in English, God bless the king of Scotland. He then unfolded a long parchment and clearing his throat, began to read out the Queen's genealogy from the first known king of Scotland to the present day. this was followed by the commencement of the second part of the religious ceremony when all the seated guests, including Richard, rose to their feet, and which began with the archbishop of St Andrews anointing the queen with holy oil on Mary's forehead, breast and hands and then as the monk's began to sing a hymn of praise, the archbishop, holding aloft the glittering crown slowly lowered it onto Mary's head to the shouts of ' God bless Queen Mary' from the assembled company whose enthusiasm almost drowned out the sound of the monk's singing and another fanfare of trumpets.

A few moments later, Mary carefully arose from the historic stone clasping both the Orb and the Sceptre and joined by Richard who smiled at her reassuringly, they began the slow walk down the hill then entered the abbey to the sound of the organ thundering out an introit as they progressed down the nave towards the High Altar where they would hear Mass.

Afterwards, with the crown once more encircling her forehead, Mary faced the congregation and calling for her son, Prince James, she took the little boy by the hand and announced.

'My lords, we present to you our son, Prince James, whom this day we create Duke of Rothesay and your future king.'

To the cheers of the assembly, Mary and Richard each holding a hand of the slightly bewildered young prince, retraced their steps down the nave and left the abbey and entered the adjoining palace where they presided over a sumptuous banquet to round off a never to be forgotten coronation day.

# 31

Richard and Mary had previously discussed at length the decision to endow James as duke of Rothesay, the traditional title for the heir to the Scottish throne, and decided that her coronation day would be the most appropriate time to make the announcement. Richard also decided to create him Prince of Wales when they made a stop in York on their return journey to London. This journey would not commence until the onset of spring when hopefully, the weather would make travel possible. Meanwhile, the court would take up residence for the winter at the mighty Stirling Castle, brooding high atop its hill above the town and nearby Bannockburn, scene of king Robert the Bruce's great victory over the English forces of king Edward II back in 1314.

Richard was fascinated by all the minute details of the battle as related to him by the earl of Angus and other Scottish nobles as he toured the battlefield and asked many questions about the life of and times of the Bruce who although as an English descendant of the defeated Edward 11, he readily conceded that the Bruce was indeed a great warrior whom he could relate to adding, 'As our two nations are now united in matrimony, let us hope and pray that we will never again be drawn into war and that we will be forever united in peace from this time onwards.'

Both Scots and Englishmen present nodded in agreement and there were many handshakes and friendly slapping on backs as they dispersed at the end of the visit.

It was Christmas Eve and winter welcomed in the Yule time season with blizzards that left great piles of snow stacked up around the castle that cut it off from the town below making any kind of travel impossible. Consequently, Christmas Day was celebrated quietly with fewer guests than usual seated in the great hall warmly dressed to keep out the draughts that lifted the heavy tapestries from the walls and almost blew out the fires located at each end of the hall from the gale force winds that howled loudly outside.

Seated at the low tables near the doors at the rear of the hall reserved for the servants not on duty, Tom Murgatroyd moaned to his long suffering wife, 'I thought that Yorkshire was bloody cold in winter but this draughty 'ole beats it hands down.'

'Oh stop yer grizzling,' Jeanie dug him sharply in the ribs with her elbow. 'It's no that bad. I have known a lot worse. Stuff yer face and enjoy the food, after all it *is* Christmas.'

'I don't care. I 'ave chilblains where I shoudn't 'ave em and that's one 'ell of a draught coming from under that soddin' door.'

'Never mind, Laddie,' Jeanie laughed at her husband's woebegone expression.' We have Hogmanay to look forward to in a few weeks. If that dinna bring a smile to yer miserable face, well nothing will.'

'What the 'ell is Hogmanay?' Tom asked, while wrapping his cloak tightly around him.

'Dinna tell me that ye have never heard of Hogmanay?' Jeanie shook her head in disbelief, much to the amusement of her fellow scots sitting nearby.

'Ye will have to forgive him, Lads and Lasses,' she explained to them. 'My husband is a puir Sassenach who doesna ken how ter welcome in the New Year.'

'Why didn't yer say it means New Year's Eve?' asked Tom raising his goblet, downing his ale and loudly belching. 'Well, whatever it is it can't be worse than today.'


It was a miracle, everyone said when New Year's Eve dawned to find that the blizzards had finally blown themselves out leaving a calm, cold day with a pale wintry sun shining on the rooftops and as darkness began to descend, bright twinkling stars appeared lighting the castle and the town at its feet in an almost magical glow.

Inside the castle Richard stood with his back to the blazing fire as Tom added the finishing touches to his new garb for the evening's upcoming celebrations. Resplendent in the Yorkist colours of murrey and blue, Richard inclined his head as Tom removed the heavy gold chain of sunnes and roses from its cushion and placed it carefully over the king's shoulders. He then offered to him his golden circlet that he had worn around his helm at Bosworth,

Richard reached out and rested it upon his brow, stepped back and asked with a grin. 'Well, Tom, will I pass muster with the Scots?'

'Aye, your grace. Yon circlet looks grand but your real crown would look even better.'

'The crown of England must remain in England,' Richard frowned. 'As her grace's crown will stay here when we return south.'

'I beg your pardon, Sire ' Tom looked suitably mollified. 'I spoke out of turn '

'Oh, put your face straight, Tom,' laughed Richard restored to good humour. 'Humility does not become you.'

Richard and Mary entered the great hall accompanied by Mary's daughter, Elizabeth, now raised to the rank of princess following her mother's accession to the throne, and Prince James, to the usual sound of trumpets and amidst the scraping of benches on the floor as the waiting guests rose to their feet. Mary was as richly attired as her husband and complimented him in matching murrey and blue and topped by the royal crown of Scotland ablaze with jewels. The royal family reached their seats but first knelt as the Archbishop of St Andrews gave a blessing. They then seated themselves and as with another fanfare, the feasting began and as course followed course the merriment grew thanks to the copious amounts of whisky consumed. So by the time the final course had ended and the trestles removed to clear the hall for dancing, most of the guests were very merry indeed. Especially the English who unlike their Scottish counterparts, were unused to the potent power of the free flowing aqua vitae.

The master of Ceremonies entered the hall armed with his mace and marching up to where the King and Queen sat on their throne like chairs, he announced with a deep bow, 'Your graces, my lords, ladies and gentlemen, prey let the reels begin.'

He loudly stamped the mace three times and then to Richard's and to his fellow English guests amazement, the sounds of the wailing of pipes and the beating of drums began to fill the hall as the doors were flung open and the musicians marched in followed by twenty colourfully garbed Highlanders each bearing a drawn sword held upright in their right hands to the cheers of the Scots.

'What is this?' Richard turned questioningly to Mary who smiling broadly replied.

'This, my dear Richard, is how we celebrate Hogmanay in Scotland. The Highlanders will begin the dancing with a reel after which display, the usual dancing will commence.'

The pipes and drums lined both sides of the hall as the highlanders halted and saluted the royal couple. Then Mary's voice rang out, 'Let the reel commence.'

Richard and the rest of the English guests watched in fascination as the dancers split into groups of four, laid down their swords with the tips touching to form a cross. The pipes and drums began to play a lively air and with both arms raised aloft, the men began to dance over the crossed swords to the whoops and whistles from the Scots that were soon joined in by the English.

'I have never seen anything like this before' Laughed Richard, joining in the clapping and urging his friends to do the same.

'I take it that you approve of our Hogmanay customs then, husband?' Mary grinned.

'Yes indeed,' he answered. 'It is wonderful and so skilful.'

Below the salt at the other end of the hall, Tom was feeling very mellow after consuming several beakers of whisky. Leaning perilously over to the other side of the bench to where Jeanie sat he slurred, 'An 'appy New Year to ye, Jeanie, my own gradely lass.'

And promptly fell head first into a bowl of potage.

The Highland dances came to an end amid the cheers and applause of the guests. The dancers saluted the king and the Queen then turned and made their way back out of the hall to a stirring march. The Master of Ceremonies once more took to the floor and announced that the dancing for everyone would now commence as the court musicians high up in the minstrels gallery tuned up their instruments. Richard and Mary rose to their feet. He bowed, kissed her hand then led her onto the floor where they were soon joined by James proudly leading his step sister, Elizabeth. Lovell and Bess followed them and they in turn were followed by as many more courtiers who were still capable of dancing.

# 32

It was mid-April before the court departed from Scotland. The time between Christmas and April had not been uneventful. Early in January, Mary had summoned parliament to meet at Stirling where she declared that she intended to grant the Crown Matrimonial to Richard with immediate effect. This news was received in stunned silence for a few moments before the assembly erupted into uproar much to Mary's dismay with the cries of 'Nay ' drowning out the 'Ayes' as the Speaker called repeatedly for order. When things eventually returned to some semblance of normality, Mary spoke again.

'My lords,' she began tight lipped with barely suppressed anger, 'what is your objection to my noble husband being granted the right to rule alongside myself?'

'Because he is an Englishman, That is why,' spat out a loud voice from the rear.

'Come forward and show yourself, Sirrah.' Mary called back as a heavily built man of middle years with long unkempt grey hair that partly hid a long jagged scar on his right cheek that ran down from below his eye to his chin, pushed his way to the front.

'Your name, Sirrah?' Mary asked coldly.

'I am Walter Ker of Cessford in the Borderlands, your grace,' he replied with an awkward bow. And pointing to his scar with a grubby finger continued. 'I got this defending Scotland from the invading English army led by yon king Richard back in 1482. *That's* why we canna have a Sassenach king.'

'My husband was not king at that time but duke of Gloucester and he was merely obeying the command of his royal brother, king Edward,' Mary retorted, growing more angry by the minute.

'Aye, your grace,' another member called out. 'And the duke, as his grace was then, gave orders that there was to be no looting, burning or any other violence when he and his army entered Edinburgh.'

There was much muttering and nodding of heads until the speaker ordered them to vote on the motion. The result proved to be very close with the 'Nays' emerging as the winners by a mere twenty votes.

Later, in the privacy of their chamber, a furious Mary informed Richard, 'That the parliament had not heard the last of this matter.'

'Let it rest for now, Marie,' he counselled her. 'There is no hurry and I have more than enough to occupy my time ruling England.'

'But you do not deserve to be so slighted. I am truly ashamed of my fellow scots and I will *not* forget this insult.'

Richard placed his arm around her shoulder and squeezed it gently. 'And I do not deserve *you.*'


The bells of York Minster rang out joyfully on a chilly Sunday morning as Richard and Mary entered through the great West door followed by their retinue to hear High Mass. hey had passed the previous two nights at Sheriff Hutton on their long journey south from Scotland and later in the afternoon, Richard invested his son James as Prince of Wales in a colourful ceremony at the Guildhall attended by the Mayor and other civic dignitaries followed by a procession through the city streets where James, wearing his coronet and Purple Velvet robe trimmed with ermine and carrying his sceptre, walked proudly between his smiling parents as they acknowledged the cheers from the watching crowds as they passed by. Richard found it increasingly difficult to smile as the walk progressed, overwhelmed as he was by poignant memories of the day when he and Anne had done the same walk with their young son, Edward, when he also had been invested as Prince of Wales. He felt tears well up in his eyes and quickly brushed them aside and smiled reassuringly at Mary who was watching him anxiously.

'Are you alright, Richard? '

'I am fine,' he answered her. 'Just a bit of a twinge in my back.'

But Mary was far from convinced and had a shrewd idea of what really troubled him and felt a pang of sympathy but said nothing further.

Later, just before the hour of vespers, Richard, accompanied by Francis Lovell, made his way quietly and without any ceremony, back to the Minster and with their footsteps echoing on the stone flagged floor, entered the royal chantry where work had begun on two of three elaborately carved tombs below the altar. The central tomb would be Richard's own and was almost complete with his effigy bearing an excellent likeness to him. He was depicted wearing his crown and with his hands folded in prayer and wearing full armour with a tabard bearing the arms of England and his personal badge of the white Boar. And his feet resting on a large Hound that, though as yet incomplete, bore a striking resemblance to Rex.

'Do you know the name of the Mason responsible for carving my effigy?' Richard asked the Dean, who was hovering anxiously in the background.

'I believe, your grace, that the Mason is a Master Broom. Does your grace wish me to send for him?'

'No, I thank you Dean, but that will not be necessary.'

A knowing smile played around Richard's lips as he ran his hand over the Hound's head before turning to inspect the tomb on his left which was now complete and bore a lifelike figure of his beloved first wife, Anne Neville. Anne had actually died in Westminster and was buried temporarily in the Abbey there and Richard planned to reinter her here in York now that her tomb was completed. The tomb on his right would eventually be the resting place of Mary and was still waiting for work to commence on it and side by side against the wall to the right of the altar were the burial places of his son, Edward and Mary's son, Robert, marked by fine marble slabs.

Suddenly changing his mind, Richard addressed the Dean once more. 'On second thoughts, Dean, I have decided that I wish to speak to Master Broom after all. Pray summon him '

'At once. your grace.' Bowing obsequiously, he turned and scurried across the yard to where the workmen were housed in temporary accommodation. Richard watched as the Dean shuffled panting on his way before saying to Lovell.

'Do you recall the eve before Bosworth when I spoke to a young lad who was my bastard son, Frank? '

'Yes, Dickon, I do. I have often wondered what became of him after the battle.'

'Well, Frank, wonder no more because you are about to meet once again.'

Lovell's eyes opened wide with surprise and he let out a long low whistle. 'Phew!, Dickon. You mean that the Mason who carved out your effigy is the same lad then?'

'Yes, the same, Frank, and I am very proud of him.' Richard paused momentarily before continuing. 'I must ask you to keep all this to yourself, Frank. Young Richard prefers anonymity '

'Of course, Dickon. It goes without saying that you have my word.'

A discreet cough announced the Dean's return accompanied by the young man in question who immediately fell to his knees on seeing Richard.

'Master Broom, if it please your grace.'

'Thank you, Dean. you may leave us now.'

The Dean bowed and backed out of the chamber as Lovell was about to speak when Richard held up his hand and waited until the Dean's footsteps had receded into the distance before he turned and raised his son to his feet.

'How are you, lad?' he asked, standing back and eyeing him from head to foot.

'I am very well, Sire, and I hope that you are also.'

'I am all the better for seeing you,' Richard smilingly turned to Lovell who still looked dazed with shock. 'Frank, here is my son, Richard Broom, and Richard, meet my oldest and most trusted friend, Viscount Lovell.'

'I am most pleased to meet you, Master Broom.'

'I am honoured, my lord,' they both answered shaking hands warmly.

'You have done excellent work on my effigy, Richard, even if you have flattered me somewhat,' Richard laughed. 'But tell me, how on earth did you manage to capture my hound's likeness so accurately?'

'Well, sire, I remember seeing your hound with you the last time we met, here in York and when I was informed that your grace wished to be depicted with a hound at your feet, I just guessed that you would like it to be him, sire.'

'You are a son to be proud of,' murmured Richard, deeply moved. Clearing his throat with a cough, he continued, 'And although my friend here now knows about you, I can assure you that on one else is aware of you and that he is the soul of discretion.'

Lovell nodded in agreement. 'Aye, Master Broome, my lips are sealed.'

Richard suddenly slapped his forehead and beaming exclaimed, 'I have just got an idea of how we can keep in touch with each other, lad, discreetly of course. Frank here can be our go between. He can write to you on my behalf and vice versa and no one will be any the wiser. Are you both agreeable? '

Both young Richard and Lovell smiled their assent and all three of them shook hands on it.

# 33

Soon after Richard and Mary had returned to Westminster they received news that saddened, but not altogether surprised them.

Richard's beloved mother, Cecily, duchess of York, was gravely ill at her residence, Berkhamstead Castle in Hertfordshire. She had reached the grand old age of eighty years and they were informed that time was rapidly running out for her. They set out immediately, accompanied by as many of Cecily's numerous grandchildren as possible including James, Richard and Anne and Bess.

On their arrival they found Cecily in bed propped up at her insistence by many pillows. Richard was shocked by her changed appearance. This once vital, proud and beautiful woman known in her youth as the Rose of Raby after her birthplace in Co Durham, had shrunk to a shadow of her former self. Wisps of thin white hair escaped from her nightcap and her hollowed cheeks accentuated her laboured breathing. The only remnant surviving from her past beauty were her eyes that still glowed and missed nothing in her changed face. Those same eyes lit up with pleasure as Richard entered her bedchamber and knelt at her bedside taking her cold blue veined hands in his warm ones and kissing them gently

'Oh, Richard, my dearest son,' she breathed softly, 'I knew that you would come.'

'Aye, my lady mother,' he murmured gently kissing her forehead. 'Nothing would have kept me away.'

'Hold me, my son,' Cecily struggled to sit up further so Richard sat on the bed and wrapped his arm around her as Mary approached and also kissed her mother – in –law on the forehead.

'Mary, my daughter. You have been as a true daughter to me and a good and loving wife to my Richard.' A sudden bout of coughing overtook her before Cecily continued with an effort, 'For which I thank you.'

'There is no need to thank me, *Maman,*' whispered Mary, with tears in her eyes. 'It is not hard to love Richard and you have been not only a mother, but a friend to me since I first arrived in England.'

Kissing Cecily again, Mary moved away to allow Bess to say a tearful goodbye to her grandmother followed by all the other grandchildren present. The youngest amongst them not really understanding what was happening.

As the evening shadows began to fall on that day, the 31 May 1495, Cecily received the last rites and just an hour later she drew her last breath lovingly held in Richard's arms. He closed her eyes, kissed her and crossing himself, gently laid her down before hastily quitting the chamber to grieve in private.

Richard led the mourners when a month later, Cecily was finally laid to rest beside her late husband, the duke of York, also named Richard, and their son, Edmund, earl of Rutland, in the York family mausoleum in the parish church at Fotheringhay, close to their castle of the same name in Northamptonshire.


Once back in Westminster, following a series of discussions, Richard and Mary decided that an alliance with Spain would be advantageous for both England and for Scotland and provide a bulwark against France whom they had good reason not to trust.

France and Scotland in the past had always been close allies but the political map of Europe had changed when the queen consort of England became the Queen Regnant of Scotland.

Wasting no further time, negotiations via the Spanish Ambassador with Queen Isabella and king Ferdinand for the hand of their ten year old daughter, the Infanta Catalina of Aragon to nine year old James opened and were concluded to the satisfaction of both parties. The betrothal was announced between the young prince and princess and it was agreed that the princess would depart for England the following spring when the marriage would take place soon after her arrival.

When news of the betrothal reached the French court, rumbles of discontent and veiled threats were hurled across the channel but were soon countermanded by similar threats issued from Spain to neighbouring France if they dared to interfere in the coming alliance.

Meanwhile, life in England continued normally as the court moved to Windsor to escape the outbreak of the sweating sickness caused by the excessive heat of summer made worse by London's filthy streets and the evil smelling Thames.

One morning, as Richard began dictating a missive to Secretary Kendall, he was suddenly distracted from the business in hand by shouts of laughter coming through the open casement from the garden outside. Exasperated by the noise, he strode to the casement where an unexpected spectacle met his amazed gaze. It was Rex, his front paws grimly clutching the rear quarters of Bess' white Poodle, Lady, as the bitch tried her best to escape from Rex's determined grip. The noise was caused by James, Richard and Anne howling with laughter as they watched Tom Murgatroyd vainly attempting to separate the two dogs.

'Oh, look, my lord father,' Little Anne cried as she caught sight of her father looking out. 'Look at Rex and Lady. They are dancing.'

'I have never heard it called that before' Richard murmured to Kendall with a grin. 'But I am glad to see that there is life in the old dog yet.'

But this event proved to be Rex's swan song. Two months later at the end of September when the court was back at Middleham, ten year old Rex peacefully passed away during the night, ensconced in his usual place at the foot of the royal bed. A tearful Tom watched by an equally saddened Richard and Mary, buried Rex in his favourite strip of garden in the inner courtyard where he would usually be found lying panting in the sun with his tongue lolling out.

'Rest in peace, owd lad,' whispered Tom, wiping away a furtive tear as he placed the last clod of earth over the grave.

'Amen to that' Richard echoed as an unashamedly weeping Mary nodded in agreement. Just then wee Hamish suddenly appeared and sensing their sorrow, the little dog ran up to them, his tail wagging slowly.

'But we still have this little fellow,' Richard bent over and scooping him up, placed him in Mary's arms.


Christmas that year was a somewhat muted affair held at Sheriff Hutton where Richard had presided over the Council of the North that now also included a sizable Scottish delegation. During the first week in November, Richard had completed arrangements for the re-internment of his beloved Anne in her splendid, now completed tomb in York Minster. On the tenth of November the cortege had almost finished its long journey from Westminster Abbey where Anne had been temporarily buried, when it arrived at Bishopsthorpe on the outskirts of York where it was met by a sombre Richard, clad in deepest mourning and accompanied by his oldest friends, Francis Lovell, Rob Percy, William Catesby and Richard Ratcliffe, also dressed in deepest black and who remembered the late Queen with great affection. The procession formed and the only sounds to be heard were the trundle of the wheels of the cart bearing the coffin draped in the arms of England and the tread of the mourners feet on the cobbles as they entered York through Micklegate Bar to be greeted by the silently waiting townspeople who bowed their heads respectfully as the cortege passed by.

Inside the Minster and in the Royal Chantry, Mary, Bess, and the Archbishop of York together with various city dignitaries awaited the procession's arrival. The Minster's great bell began to toll as the cortege entered by the west door and progressed slowly to the chantry where the archbishop began the service of the re – internment. As the coffin was gently lowered into the gaping vault, Richard stepped forward, bowed, and began to slowly sprinkle a bunch of twenty eight white roses, one for each year of Anne's life onto the coffin as Mary, also clad in unrelieved black, honoured her predecessor with a deep curtsey.

# 34

The winter of 1495 - 96 proved to be one of the severest ever with heavier than usual falls of snow made worse by incessant gale force winds that whistled down all the nooks and crannies of Sheriff Hutton Castle making it almost impossible to retain any heating. This helped Richard to decide to build two new modern edifices in York.

A royal residence alongside a building to house his proposed Parliament of the North, an idea that he had been mulling over for some time

'I think that is an excellent suggestion,' Mary had agreed when he told her of his plan.

'I propose that the parliament will comprise of an equal number of both English and Scottish members that will be able to work together for the mutual benefit of both our nations '

'And as both Edinburgh and London are almost equal distances from York, it is the ideal place for the parliament ' Enthused Mary, squeezing Richard's hand.

'Exactly' He grinned, releasing his hand from her grip.

'I will begin to draw up plans immediately, I have a very good architect in mind '

Reactions when the news was announced were mixed but on the whole, favourable. Some doubts about venturing so far into England were expressed by a few Scots who were quickly reassured by Mary who explained to them the benefits of a joint government. The other main opposition came from London who feared a loss of their power and influence as the capitol city of England.

'There will be no question of that happening' Richard had declared .

'The main seat of government will always remain in Westminster. The York Assembly will mainly be concerned with matters relating to Scotland and to the north.'

With the coming of spring building work began on Richard's project. A large area beside the Guildhall and facing the river Ouse was cleared to make way for what promised to be a most impressive royal residence and parliament building. Work was well under way when the court returned to Westminster to prepare for the arrival of the young Spanish Princess.

The Spanish Galleon bearing the Infanta Catalina of Aragon, or as she would henceforth be known, Catherine, Princess of Wales, and its escorting vessels, duly arrived and safely docked at Southampton in mid-June where Richard, Mary and an apprehensive James, the young bridegroom to be, greeted her. Attended by members of her household led by her Duenna, Donna Elvira Di Silva, she stepped ashore and knelt to the king and Queen, to the cheers of the curious onlookers, all excited at their first glimpse of their future Queen.

A smiling Richard stepped forward and taking both her hands in his, gently raised her to her feet. He then welcomed her speaking in Latin and to his amazement, she replied in broken English.

'You speak English, my dear Princess?' he beamed in surprise.

'Yes, your grace' she answered shyly. 'I regret not very well as yet but I will improve with practice.'

'I am sure that you will. I can see that you are a very determined young lady.'

He led her to Mary who took her in her arms and kissed her on both cheeks and then it was James' turn to greet his betrothed. Although a year younger than Catherine, he already stood taller. At his father's instigation and blushing furiously, he bowed and kissed her hand as she dropped a curtsey to him.

'The Princess is a pleasant looking girl is she not?' Richard whispered to Mary as they watched James offer his hand to Catherine who smiling demurely, placed her hand on his.

'Yes indeed,' Mary agreed. 'She is by no means a great beauty but seems good natured and her studying of English is to be commended.'

The two children, still hand in hand, bowed and curtseyed to the king and to the Queen before following them to where a comfortably upholstered litter awaited Mary and Catherine. Mary entered the litter followed by Catherine who sat beside her with her eyes cast down. Mary, glancing at the clearly nervous young girl, smiled reassuringly.

'I hope that you will be happy with us, Catherine. I am sure that you will be once you get to know us.'

'Your grace is very kind,' Catherine replied with a quick smile that lit up her whole face, completely transforming it.

Richard and James rode on either side of the litter acknowledging the cheers of the crowds lining the streets as they rode to their overnight lodgings before beginning their long journey back to Westminster the following day.

One month later on a beautiful summer's day, the Prince and the Princess were married in Westminster Abbey. Both children were attired in clothing of rich white satin. Catherine's gown and headdress in traditional Spanish style with a long filmy veil that trailed behind her almost hiding her light brown hair that fell in waves to just below her waist while James' garb was highlighted by the wearing of his Prince of Wales coronet that gleamed brightly in the light from the of hundreds of candles that lit the abbey and from the rays of the sun that streamed colourfully through the windows.

'Och, Tom, will you look at those wee bairns,' sniffed Jeanie wiping her eyes and looking down from their privileged seats high above the altar. 'Doesna it touch ye here?' she whispered, pointing to her heart.

'Nay, woman' Tom shrugged. 'It's all down to bloody politics. Them there young 'uns are just pawns in an old game,' he sniffed turning his head away so that his wife would not see the tear in his eye.

The weeks following the royal wedding were fairly uneventful. The new Princess of Wales soon settled down with her new family and to the relief of Richard and Mary, a close bond of friendship was quickly forged between James and Catherine that augured well for their future lives together. Taking advantage of the relative calm, Richard introduced many new laws to the advantage of the commons whose lives he gradually made much easier while slowly subtly, reducing the power of the nobles, saying that, 'England must never again have a so called 'Kingmaker,' while Mary instigated a similar policy in Scotland but with less success. Richard's innovations made him very popular with the ordinary working men and women and he was loudly greeted by cheers and whistles whenever he ventured out in public.

# 35

However, trouble was not far off the horizon. The first hint of the gathering storm came to light just after the Easter of 1497 when the court was in residence in Edinburgh. An envoy from the king of Denmark requested an audience with Mary which was granted. The man knelt on one knee before her and handed her a sealed missive from his king in which he requested the return to Danish rule, the islands of Orkney and of Shetland that had formed the dowry of the Danish Princess Margaret on her marriage to king James III in 1469. The Danish excuse being that as Queen Margaret and her children were all now deceased the islands should revert to Denmark.

'But this is monstrous,' Mary raged to Richard when they were alone in the privacy of their chamber. 'The islands were only part of my sister- in-law's dowry. They were surety for the sum of 10.000 crowns which the Danes could not afford at the time of the marriage and which they have NEVER paid.'

'Then as far as I can see, the islands are now part of Scotland and should remain so,' answered Richard thoughtfully.

'Indeed they shall and I will make our position abundantly clear at tomorrow's audience,' resolved Mary.

The following day, with Richard seated beside her this time, Mary received the envoy and handed to him a sealed missive addressed to the Danish king.

'With much consideration we have concluded that the islands of Orkney and of Shetland, because of the Danish failure to pay the late Queen's dowry, the islands by default, belong to Scotland and will remain so,' Mary informed the envoy coldly. 'All is explained in this document for you to give to your king. '

'My King and fellow countrymen will not be pleased with your grace's answer,' the envoy, looking nonplussed, replied. 'It could even lead to war between our two nations.'

Richard, who had up to now been a silent witness to the exchange of words, suddenly interrupted the envoy in full flow.

'You are wrong there, my friend,' he stated quietly but with a clear meaning. 'If war is declared on Scotland, it will have declared war on England also. Our two nations now stand together and make no mistake, any threat to Scotland is also a threat to England so consider that carefully when you speak so lightly of war.'

The envoy was visibly startled by Richard's intervention and clutching the missive to his breast, bowed awkwardly as the king and Queen arose from their seats and quit the audience chamber.

Richard had originally planned to return to Westminster following the Easter celebrations but due to the threat of hostilities in Scotland, decided to remain north of the border to await any future developments while at the same time sending an urgent message south to the Duke of Norfolk in London to assemble the fleet and to prepare to sail north to intercept any Danish invasion of Scotland. Meanwhile, Mary summoned an emergency meeting of parliament in which she called upon the lowland lords and the Highland clan chiefs to forget their long held mistrust of each other and to band together to defend their homeland.

At Mary's invitation, Richard also addressed the assembly where he pledged the help of the large English garrison at Berwick-Upon-Tweed should it be needed. He also offered his own personal sword to help defend his wife's throne. The offer of English help was treated warily in some quarters, especially by the Borderers whose distrust of their English counterparts on their side of the border had festered for generations. To reassure them, Richard gave his solemn word that no English army would enter Scotland unless they were invited to do so by parliament. This pledge met with nods of approval from most of the members who were impressed by Richard's sincerity.

The fleet of forty warships under the command of Thomas Howard, Duke of Norfolk, had dropped anchor off Scarborough when disturbing news began to filter through that France, angered that the Scottish/English marriage had broken the traditional 'Auld Alliance' between them, had, in revenge, allied themselves with Denmark and promised to assist them with men and ships in their planned invasion of Scotland.

Richard wasted no time on receiving this threatening news and riding hard for York, summoned the newly formed Anglo/Scottish Parliament to meet him there without delay. Once assembled, he informed them of the increased danger threatened by the French intervention.

There was uproar and consternation at the news quickly followed by anger, especially from the Scots who felt betrayed by their old allies.

'What can we do?' the members cried in dismay.

'My lords,' bellowed the Speaker, banging his staff of office on the floor for silence. 'Order, Order. Pray silence for his grace to continue.'

'Thank you, Master Speaker,' shouted Richard above the din.

The uneasy rumbling eventually became a low murmuring as Richard continued.

'My lords, rest assured the French fleet will not reach Scotland intact. They will be harried by the guns and ships of the English enclave at Calais who will follow them across the Channel and up into the North Sea where the main English fleet awaits them at Scarborough, as does the Scottish fleet further north.' Richard raised a clenched fist to emphasise his point.

'My lords, if they make it as far as Scarborough, they will be destroyed like rats in a trap.' Richard's fist crashed loudly onto the table before him as he paused for breath before continuing.

'Any stragglers will be blown to Hell by the guns at Berwick as will any Danes encountered making for Scotland.'

Richard's impassioned speech was greeted by applause and he was relieved to see that the Scottish Delegation were the most enthusiastic in their cheers.

'I think that you have won the Scots over at last, Dickon,' beamed Lovell a few minutes later, joining Richard in downing a cool tankard of ale. 'And about time, too, ' he added wiping his fingers across his wet mouth.

'We haven't defeated our enemies yet, Frank,' Richard replied soberly. 'When we have, that will be the time to congratulate ourselves.'

Richard returned north, taking up residence at Berwick Castle where he was joined by Mary to wait upon events. They had been there for a month, a month taken up with preparations for war when word reached them that the French fleet was reported to have been seen off the coast of Norfolk hotly pursued by the smaller fleet from Calais commanded by the Captain of Calais, Richard's bastard son, Sir John of Pontefract. Latest news from Richard's efficient network of scouts reported that a skirmish had taken place off Cromer in which the larger French fleet had emerged victorious but with losses on both sides. Richard waited anxiously for news of his son and was relieved to learn that his badly damaged vessel had managed to limp as far as the Thames estuary and to drop anchor there. And although he had sustained a slight injury to his leg, John was otherwise unhurt.

The main fleet at anchor at Scarborough was alerted that the French ships were approaching them at the same time news reached Richard that a Danish armada had been spotted setting a course and was heading towards a rendezvous with its French allies. Richard acted quickly, alerting the smaller but efficient Scottish Navy under the command of Sir Donald Maclean, who were anchored off the entrance to the Firth of Forth at North Berwick, to follow the Danes at a safe distance but *not* to engage with them until the French and the Danes were trapped between the English to the south and themselves to the north of them.

Richard's strategy worked. The Commanders of the cumbersome French Galleys were utterly dismayed when the much lighter English fleet emerged out of a convenient fog that had suddenly descended just off Whitby, and began following them up the coast but could not understand why the English ships made no attempt to fire upon them.

Then, as dawn broke two days later on what promised to be a calm summer's morn, a lookout in the crow's nest of the leading French galley, spotted the first of the Danish ships on the horizon sailing towards them and making good time with the wind at their backs. As the light increased, more Danish vessels appeared much to the relief of the French. But their joyfulness was brief as to their utter dismay, the Scottish fleet suddenly hove into view behind the Danes closing in on them rapidly.

'Mon Dieu!' screamed the French commander, wildly waving his arms.

'We are trapped between the Scots and the cursed English. What is that landfall over yonder?'

'I believe that is the place they call Berwick, Monseigneur,' answered one of his Captains.

'Then we are truly doomed.' He shook his head in despair. Then brightening up, he ordered word to be sent to all the fleet that for the honour of France, they would fight unto the death.

Meanwhile, thanks to a series of beacons that Richard had instituted every three miles up the east coast from London to the border. He was kept fully aware of the exact French position as they progressed north, so he was ready and waiting early that morning at first light high on the castle battlements. Waiting alongside him were his most trusted and experienced battle commanders led by Rob Percy, Richard Ratcliffe and Francis Lovell.

Although no one mentioned it, on a day like this one, they all missed the bluff presence of Sir Ralph de Assheton, known as the Black Knight because of the colour of his armour.

The tough old warrior had fought beside them at Bosworth only to be shot dead a year later in his home in Lancashire by a disgruntled tenant.

As the last of the early morning haar lifted from over the castle, an amazing sight greeted Richard and his commanders as obeying their orders, the Scots and the English vessels formed a wide circle around the enemy ships making it impossible for them to escape.

Richard signalled the trumpeters high on the ramparts to loudly sound the attack. After what seemed like a long time to the watchers on the battlements and in the town of Berwick below, but which was actually only a matter of minutes, the air was suddenly rent by the roar of cannon fired from both the castle and on the ships as they began to assail each other. The English and the Scots began to slowly but surely close in on their enemy's vessels, forcing them ever closer so that their guns began to blaze into each other, toppling masts and ramming together with a terrible grinding noise added to the screams of agony from the injured and the dying aboard the now sinking ships.

Some wounded men attempted to make land clinging on to pieces of debris while the uninjured tried to swim ashore but they were met by a hail of arrows fired from the castle battlements until the shore was dotted by the dead and the dying caught in the deadly crossfire.

By noon it was all over. The losses sustained by both the French and the Danes was phenomenal whilst the victorious English and Scots losses were minimal A few of the enemy ships that were still capable of sailing began to drift away, most of them listing badly to one side but these were soon overtaken by the allied fleet and brutally sunk.

News of the great victory spread like wildfire through the town and over the border into Scotland where with the realisation that the threat of invasion had passed, hordes of jubilant Scots crossed the border and poured into Berwick's narrow streets shouting for, 'Guid King Richard.' They were soon joined by the townsfolk as they clamoured outside the castle's walls, while inside the castle Richard was cheered by the enthusiastic garrison and clapped on the back by his old comrades-in-arms.

Mary ran up to him, throwing her arms around his neck and kissed him soundly on the mouth.

'Thank you, oh thank you, Richard. You have saved Scotland and we will always be grateful to you,' she breathed into his ear then to the cheers of the onlookers, kissed him again.

'For thanks such as this, Marie,' he smiled, feeling the tension from the battle drain away, 'I would do battle for you every day,' he whispered as he returned her kisses.

As evening approached towards the end of that memorable day. The tide began to turn inland carrying the grim evidence of the battle in the shape of dead men, boys, and horses being washed ashore together with debris in the form of weaponry and parts of the sunken ships that cluttered the beaches for miles on either side of Berwick. A massive clean-up was instigated but it was to be many days before the last of the debris was washed ashore and the dead given Christian burial.

# 36

Richard and Mary returned to Edinburgh and were given a rapturous reception by the townspeople led by the Provost whose address of welcome was drowned out by the cheers and the firing in salute of the cannons high up above the city on the castle ramparts, as they rode down the Royal Mile accompanied by the princes James and Richard both on horseback and by the princesses, Anne, Elizabeth and Catherine in an ornately decorated litter before drawing to a halt at St Giles Cathedral to attend a service of thanksgiving for the victory before continuing on to Holyrood Palace led by marching Highlanders triumphantly playing the pipes and drums.

The royal procession was followed by a contingent of English Archers and Sailors marching alongside their Scottish counterpoints which caused Richard Ratcliffe to remark to Lovell riding beside him.

'What a day, Frank, never did I expect to hear English soldiers being cheered by the Scots.'

'Nor did I, Dick,' Lovell laughed, deftly catching a flower tossed by a grinning young woman. 'This day will surely go down in history.'

The mood of elation continued and in the days that followed, the Royal family were feted everywhere they visited during a whistle stop tour with a stop first at Linlithgow Palace followed by Falkirk, Cumbernauld and eventually returned to another enthusiastic welcome in Edinburgh.

Two days later a delegation from the Parliament led by the Speaker, the earls of Angus and Bothwell and the archbishop of St Andrews, humbly requested an audience with their graces the queen and her royal husband on a matter of great importance.

Their curiosity thoroughly aroused by the seriousness of the unexpected request, Mary and Richard received the large delegation in the great chamber with both seated on throne like chairs of state. The delegation entered and approaching the sovereigns, they all fell to their knees. Mary then addressed them, bidding them to rise and to state their business. The Speaker stepped forward and his voice rang out loudly as he began.

'Your grace, I speak on behalf of your loyal parliament and the lords and commons of your realm of Scotland and the Isles to request that the noble King Richard, your grace's royal husband, will, with your consent, accept with our gratitude the Crown Matrimonial of Scotland for saving your kingdom from invasion by the Danes and the French.'

This unexpected announcement caused a gasp of amazement from the onlookers only to be silenced by Mary raising her hand before replying after receiving a barely perceptive nod of agreement from Richard.

'My lords, I am pleased that at last you appreciate the debt of gratitude that Scotland owes to my dear husband and that you now see fit to offer to him the Crown Matrimonial that you had previously refused to grant to him. However, the decision to accept or to refuse your offer rests solely with his grace the King.'

She gestured to Richard who rose slowly to his feet and with a bow, took his wife's hand in his and kissed it before turning to face the delegation with his usual air of quiet dignity that never failed to impress his audiences.

'My lords,' he began, his voice low timbered but that never the less, carried to every corner of the large chamber. 'I thank you for the honour that you have bestowed upon me this day and I gladly accept your offer of the Crown Matrimonial of Scotland '

Loud cheers and the stamping of feet greeted his announcement but holding up his hand for silence, Richard continued, 'And furthermore,' he paused until the last of the applause ebbed away and then resumed, 'I give you my solemn pledge that I will continue to defend Scotland from the threats of any future enemies and will honour and uphold the laws of this land and will defer to her grace Queen Mary in all matters relating to her kingdom.'

More applause and whistles rang out and at a signal from the Archbishop, two acolytes entered the chamber, one bearing an ornate copy of the Holy Bible while his companion bore on a crimson velvet cushion, the crown of Scotland.

The delegates parted down the centre of the chamber to allow the acolytes a clear passage until they halted before a small table that had been hastily placed before the archbishop, the king and the queen. The Bible was placed on the table first and then the Crown was laid atop it. The archbishop then stepped up to the table followed by Richard who stood directly opposite to him and who then placed his right hand on the crown as the archbishop intoned.

'My lord king, Do you solemnly swear before God and everyone here present to uphold the laws and customs of Scotland and of the Isles, so help you God?'

'I do so solemnly swear, So help me God,' Richard swore before crossing himself.

'Your grace, would you please kneel?' asked the archbishop lifting the crown from its cushion.

Richard knelt and the archbishop placed the crown briefly upon Richard's head before replacing it back upon the cushion. Richard rose to his feet as Mary came to stand beside him and reaching up laid her hands on his shoulders then kissed him on both cheeks to the loud applause and the cheers of both the Scottish and the English onlookers.

Later, after the last of the day's solemnity's were finished and Richard and Mary were returning to their private chambers, Richard was overwhelmed by congratulations from individual courtiers and laughed quite happily at some witty remarks from his old friends in private as they took advantage of their years of closeness. He was especially amused by Rob Percy's suggestion that.

'I expect you will take to wearing the kilt and be learning to play the pipes now eh, Dickon? '

To which Richard Ratcliffe retorted. 'Don't be daft, Rob. How could Dickon manage to mount his horse in a high wind without showing off his crown jewels to all the gawping watchers? '

'Enough, lads, enough,' Richard laughed. 'It has been a long day and it is time that we were all abed so off you all go.'

Richard straightened himself upwards, furtively rubbing his lower back that was paining him as the memorable day drew towards its close. As his still guffawing friends closed the chamber door behind them, he let out a huge sigh of relief that much as he appreciated their humour, all he wanted to do was to be able to relax with a cup of wine and a hot brick at his back before joining Mary in their bedchamber.

Anticipating his needs like the good body servant that he was, Tom Murgatroyd was ready and waiting with a flagon of wine and the hot brick inside its woollen pouch.

'Thank you, Tom.' Easing himself into his chair by the fire, Richard took a sip of the wine as Tom placed the brick at his back in exactly the right place to bring him more ease.

Prince, son of Richard's late beloved Rex, but a much quieter hound, padded across the chamber softly, his paws hardly making a sound, as he laid his head on his master's knee, his wagging tail thumping the floor as Richard tickled him behind his ears.

As Tom fussed around him, Richard could not help but notice that his long time servant was trying hard, not very successfully, to suppress his amusement at something.

'Come on, Tom. Spit it out. What has amused you?'

'Well, Sire,' He looked down sheepishly. 'I couldn't 'elp overhearing Sir Robert asking if you would start to wear a kilt and Sir Richard's answer about you showing your arse. Begging yer pardon, Sire. I'm reet sorry, I shoudna 'ave said that but it were reet funny.'

'Well, Tom, I also found it ' Reet funny.' Now, help me into my bed gown and I will bid you goodnight.'

# 37

Events moved on swiftly following Richard's acceptance of the Crown Matrimonial. Within six months, an Act of Union between both nations had been drawn up and passed by both Parliaments. The act also guaranteed that both England and Scotland retained their own laws, customs and privileges without any interference from the other although major decisions regarding for example, the security of the nations would in future be joint decisions. One particular clause that both Richard and Mary had insisted upon was that if Richard outlived Mary, he would immediately abdicate his share of the Scottish Crown to their heir, Prince James, who would reign as king of Scots only until such time as he would also become king of England following the demise of Richard. The only exception being that if James was still a minor when succeeding to the Scottish throne, then Richard would rule until such time that his son attained his majority.

Richard and Mary returned to Westminster in time for Christmas and the New year 1498 which were celebrated on a lavish scale with feasting, drinking and dancing and entertainment by the minstrels and mummers and was heartily enjoyed by all, especially the children who, despite the freezing conditions outdoors, ran riot pelting each other with snowballs and any unlucky adults who happened to be passing by. The only ones to ignore this behaviour was James and Catherine, who thought that at their slightly older age, such pranks were below their dignity, much to the secret amusement of Richard and Mary.

With the coming of spring, they returned to Scotland and undertook a tour of the highlands where James became fascinated by the Gaelic language and expressed a wish to learn it. A fast growing young man of almost twelve, James impressed his parents with eagerness to learn all aspects of his future role as King.

'It would help me enormously in the future if I could speak to the highlanders in their own language, would it not, my lord father, my lady mother?' he asked, his eyes shining with enthusiasm.

Mary and Richard smiled at each other in mutual pride of their eldest son and heir. Tall for his age, he closely resembled Richard with the same blond hair now darkening to brown and his blue-grey eyes. With a love of book learning, but showing equal promise in the use of arms, a necessary accomplishment for a future king, he inspired his parents with great confidence for the future.

'That is an excellent idea, Jamie,' Mary enthused. 'I often wish that I could speak to the highlanders and the people of the isles in their own tongue.'

'I agree with your lady mother, lad,' nodded Richard in agreement. 'We will have to look into the matter for you.'

'Hmm,' Mary tapped her lips with her forefinger thoughtfully. 'I believe that I have the very man for the job.' Turning towards Richard she continued, 'Do you remember that huge man who showed us round the Isle of Skye, Sir Ian Mackinnon?'

'Aye, I remember him. I recall that he spoke very good English. Quite unusual I thought for someone from the Isles.'

By the time that the King and Queen had returned south of the border and were in Residence at Middleham for most of the summer, Sir Ian was firmly settled in as a member of the household.

A large jovial man with an immense head topped by a thick thatch of flaming red hair and a long beard of the same colour, he presented a somewhat fearsome appearance which belied his good nature. Not only did he tutor James in the Gaelic but anyone else who was also interested, including James' younger brother, Richard.

Young Richard was totally different from James. He was not the scholarly type at all, being more interested in outdoor pursuits such as hunting, hawking, and the acquiring of military skills. In appearance, he was nothing like either of his parents but resembled his late uncle, Edward IV, having inherited that king's blond handsome looks and also promising to match him in height when he was fully grown. But despite their different interests, the two brothers were firm friends.

While at Middleham, Richard and Mary received a surprise request from Richard's niece, Margaret of Clarence.

Three years earlier Richard had betrothed her to a Scottish Earl who had unfortunately died of the plague before the marriage had taken place. Since then, she had spent most of her time caring for her brother, Edward, who although by now a man in his twenties was still childlike.

'What can we do for you, Margaret?' Richard smiled, signalling for her to rise from her curtsey.

'If it please your graces,' Margaret began quietly, 'I have a request to make that I hope you will be able to grant.'

'What is it, niece?'

She glanced around then swallowing nervously began, 'With your consent, Uncle...' She hesitated then the words tumbled out in a hurry. 'I, I wish to take the veil. I wish to embrace the religious life.'

'Are you quite certain about this, Margaret?' Mary asked seriously as a shocked Richard appeared to be stuck for words at this totally unexpected declaration.

'I am quite sure, aunt Mary,' Margaret answered firmly. 'I believe that I have received a call from God.'

'Then you must answer it,' Richard interjected, recovering his composure. 'Have you any preference as to where you wish to take your vows?'

'With your permission, Uncle. I first heard the call in York and that is where I feel that I should take my vows.'

'Then York it shall be.'

Margaret took Richard's hand and kissed it as he patted her shoulder.

'And do not worry about Edward,' Mary interrupted. 'He will be well cared for.'


Later in the year, Elizabeth, Mary's daughter from her first marriage was married to the eldest son and heir of the Earl of Lennox in a lavish ceremony in St Giles Cathedral in Edinburgh, thus strengthening her Scottish background. Although happy with her marriage, Elizabeth wept when it was time for Richard and her mother to return to England.

'I shall miss you all so much,' she sniffed as she embraced her half siblings.

Then Richard kissed her goodbye. 'You have always been as a true daughter to me,' he told her as she wiped her eyes.

'And I could not have wished for a better father than you, my lord,' she answered him with a watery smile.

It was then time for mother and daughter to bid each other a tearful farewell with Mary promising to return to Scotland before too long.

# 38

During the late spring of 1500 Richard's long serving secretary, John Kendall, approached him with a suggestion that he hoped Richard would act upon.

'As you know, your grace, I am now getting on in years and am not as quick as I used to be'

He hesitated with a rueful smile before continuing. 'Sire, would you consider allowing me a young assistant who could eventually take over my duties when I become too old and feeble to work?'

'Why, John,' Richard grinned, 'I could never think of you as old and feeble.' He then continued seriously, 'Both you and your father before you have loyally served the House of York for more years than I care to remember. But, time catches up with all of us in the end. Do you have someone in mind?'

'Yes, Sire. He is a young Lawyer with a brilliant mind. I have known his father, a Judge, for many years. They are a well-respected London family.'

'And what pray, is the name of this young man?'

'His name, your grace, is Thomas More.'

Two days later after giving the matter some thought. Richard instructed Kendall to summon Thomas More to his presence. He watched intently as a young man with thin features and nondescript brown hair, soberly clad in a dark blue doublet and matching hose topped by a long grey Lawyers gown. His long slim fingers clutching a dark blue hat as Kendall announced.

'Master Thomas More, if it please your grace.' The young man dropped to his knees, his head bowed respectfully.

'Arise, Master More.' Richard waved a hand and as More rose to his feet he noticed the silver Crucifix that hung from a chain around the young man's neck before he hastily tucked it inside his doublet. Leaning back in his chair with his hands clasped together on the table before him, Richard studied the young man closely before asking, 'Tell me, Master More, why do you wish to become my junior Secretary?'

Without a moment's hesitation, More replied, 'Because I wish to have the honour to serve your grace in any capacity that your grace deems me worthy of.'

Richard nodded before continuing,. 'Master Kendall has informed me that you studied at Oxford and that you completed your legal training at both the New Inn and at Lincolns Inn.

'That is correct, your grace.'

'And did you not also spend some time in the Charterhouse in religious contemplation?'

'Yes, Sire, but I decided that I was too worldly for the religious life.'

'What do you mean by that?'

More flushed, losing some of his composure before replying quietly, 'I realised that sometime in the future that I would wish to have a wife and a family of my own, Sire.'

'Well, that is an honest answer, Master More. You may begin tomorrow as Master Kendall's assistant.'

Richard rose to his feet as a huge smile lit up More's somewhat serious expression as he knelt and kissed Richard's hand.

'Thank you, your grace. I promise that you will not regret my appointment.'

'I sincerely hope not,' said Richard drily. 'Master Kendall here will acquaint you with your future duties.'

Richard's decision to employ him proved to be a wise one and Thomas More soon became a valued servant of the crown.


Richard and Mary were resident in York presiding over the Anglo/Scottish Parliament on the 18th of September when a courier arrived whose mud splattered boots and travelling cloak revealed the urgency of his journey, begged an audience with the king which Richard granted while taking his ease with Francis Lovell, Robert Percy and Richard Ratcliffe before escorting Mary into the great Hall for dinner.

Recognising the courier as one based at Barnard Castle, Richard bade him rise.

'Well, Hawkins. What news do you bring? '

'May it please your grace.' He swallowed drawing breath before continuing. 'Three days ago, Bishop John Morton died unrepentant at Barnard Castle.'

Hearing which, Lovell let out a long slow whistle before saying, 'And about time too. Why, he must be about eighty. May he rot in Hell.'

'Aye, I agree with you,' Richard concurred before asking the courier, 'Prey what do you mean by unrepentant?'

'Well, Sire, when it became obvious that Morton was dying a Priest was sent for to hear his confession and to administer the last rites.'

'Yes, yes, carry on.'

'Aye, Sire, well some of us hid behind a curtain hoping to hear Morton confess to plotting with the Duke of Buckingham and the Lady Margaret Beaufort to bring the Tudor to England, but he refused to do so and so he died unrepentant.'

'Thank you, Hawkins, for bringing me the news,' said Richard. 'Has he been buried?'

'Yes, Sire, in the local churchyard in an unmarked grave. I hope that we acted correctly, your grace.'

'Yes, you did. Go now and get some food and drink and a good night's sleep before you return with my thanks to Barnard Castle.'

'Another chapter from the past now closed, Dickon,' Ratcliffe murmured quietly.

'Amen to that,' Richard agreed.

# 39

1502 was a milestone year for Richard when his daughter - in - law, Catherine, gave birth to a healthy son on the 30th June at Windsor. The young father, James, who was just two months short of his sixteenth birthday, was bursting with pride as he rode to Westminster and strode into his parents chamber without waiting to be announced to give them the good news as they sat breaking their fast.

The morning was unseasonably cool for summer with rain falling steadily but this had not deterred the young prince who was totally unaware of the puddles his dripping cloak was creating on the polished floor.

'Hell's Teeth, whatever is the matter, Jamie. Has the Thames turned into liquid gold?'

Pushing back his chair, Richard strode towards his son, clicking his fingers to a servant to remove the prince's sodden cloak before it could do more damage.

'Better than that, my lord father.' Suddenly remembering his manners, James knelt despite the puddles and grasped his father's hand as rising from her chair, Mary joined them.

'My lord and lady, I bring you great tidings. At three of the clock this morning, my dear wife gave birth to a healthy boy'

Mary and Richard looked at each other in astonishment before Mary recovering herself asked.

'But how can that be, my son? She was not due to go into confinement for at least another three weeks.'

James smiled somewhat sheepishly before replying. 'The babe is full term, my lady mother. Kate and I pre-dated our official bedding ceremony by about one month'

'You did, did you?'

And much to James' relief, Richard laughed heartily despite his attempt at seriousness.

'Kate and I love each other, father,' James answered simply.

'And we have a grandson, Richard. The succession is even more securely assured.' Mary reached up and kissed Richard's cheek before embracing her son. 'Is Catherine well?'

'She is well, my lady mother, and cannot wait to show off our son to you both.'

'Then we must celebrate without delay,' cried Richard, taking his turn to embrace James at the same time remembering that he himself had only been slightly older when he had fathered the first of his own illegitimate children.

Two days later they arrived at Windsor and Mary immediately entered the confinement chamber to find a beaming Catherine sitting up in bed rocking her baby in her arms and crooning softly to him.

'Oc! But he is a bonny wee laddie,' gushed Mary as Catherine handed him to his grandmother. 'I must introduce him to his grandfather who is waiting impatiently outside.'

'Of course, my lady mother,' Catherine smiled understandingly, fully aware that men, even a King, were not allowed to enter a confinement chamber.

'Here is your grandson, Richard.' Mary carefully placed the baby into his arms, amused at his terrified expression which quickly to wonder as the little one grasped his finger in his tiny hand.

'Are you pleased with him, my lord father?'

'How could I not be?' answered a bemused Richard, never taking his eyes from his grandson's face.

'Have you thought of a name for him, my son?' asked Mary, turning to James.

'If it pleases you, my lord father and my lady mother. Kate and I would like to name him Richard,' James replied.

'That would be highly suitable, Jamie,' Mary nodded. 'Do you not agree, Richard?'

'Yes, if that is what you want,' Richard answered, as suddenly the baby began to cry and he hastily handed him over to the hovering nurse.

'How does it feel to be a grandmother for the second time, Marie?' Richard asked, remembering that his step daughter Elizabeth had given birth to a daughter at her home in Scotland the previous year.

'Och, it is a grand feeling, my dear,' Mary smiled.

Richard's expression suddenly changed to one of seriousness with a faraway look in his eyes as he recalled a sad event known only to himself and to Francis Lovell that had occurred two years ago when the wife of his illegitimate son, Richard, died at their home at Eastwell in Kent giving birth to their son, also named Richard who only lived for a few hours before he too died leaving his father devastated and vowing never to marry again.

Richard was at Middleham with his family when on the second of October, his fiftieth birthday was celebrated in grand style with a great feast to which all his old friends and their families were invited plus all the inhabitants of the small town that had grown up around the castle who turned out in force to enjoy the spectacle. As the festivities drew to a close, Richard rose to his feet and in a short speech thanked everyone for all their gifts and good wishes which he declared he would always treasure.

As he resumed his seat to wild cheers and applause, Tom Murgatroyd tried to make himself heard to his wife above the din.

'Eeh, lass, I'm reet proud to 'ave served our King since he were a young lad of ten. I allus knew he would do us proud.'

'Aye,' Jeanie agreed. 'And doesna he look well for his age. Nobody would guess that he is fifty.'

Apart from a few extra lines around his eyes and his mouth and a smattering of grey in his hair, Richard had retained the slim figure that belied his age.

'Bah, woman,' spat Tom. 'As if his grace could give a flying fart what he looks like.'

# 40

The clouds of war were gathering momentum over France and moving ever threateningly towards the English pale around Calais.

It was a fine spring day in mid-April 1504 when Richard, who was resident in Westminster, received an urgent message from his son, Sir John of Pontefract, the Captain of Calais, urgently requesting help. Calais had always been maintained by a strong garrison to defend the last English outpost in France which the French had periodically tried to retake, so far with no success, since Calais became an outcrop of England in 1347 when won by Edward 111 during the so called one hundred years war.

This time however the French threat appeared to be more serious thanks to their king, Louis XII. John reported to his father that his spies had informed him, that a large French army was seen to be approaching from the south west and marching towards the castle of Hammes, which was situated on the edge of the pale of Calais approximately twenty miles from the port of that name.

On learning this disturbing news Richard acted speedily, well aware that John would not have sent such a message unless real danger threatened.

His first action was to call up the commanders of the levies from the southern counties and those of the midlands to assemble their men and to march without delay to Dover where he would meet them. At the same time he also summoned Thomas Howard, the Duke of Norfolk, who commanded the Navy to

'Have ready fully victualled and equipped ships of war to await myself and my army's arrival at Dover' ' It shall be done at once, your grace' Promised Norfolk.

Following two weeks of frantic preparations, Richard was ready to depart for the coast. On a clear, sun filled morning, Mary and the children stood upon the steps of Westminster Palace to bid Richard and his entourage God speed. As clad in shining silver armour topped by a silken tabard bearing the colourful arms of both England and of Scotland and topped by a golden circlet around his helm, he made an impressive figure as mounted on his great white war horse, he leaned over and first kissed the children and clasped James' shoulders in a firm grip as he instructed him.

'I place the safety of your wife, son, mother and your siblings in your hands while I am away, my son'

To which James replied.

'Rest assured, my lord, I will take care of them but, but I wish that I was going with you'

Richard sighed

'We have been over all this before, Jamie. If ought should happen to me, you will be King and must defend our two nations'

James smiled ruefully. ' I know that, father and I will pray for your safe return'

'Good lad' Richard smiled and hugged him tightly before turning to Mary and taking her into his warm embrace, kissed her hard on the mouth saying

'Farewell, Marie, my heart. I will soon return victorious, never fear'

'I don't doubt it, my love' Mary murmured, reluctant to let him go. 'Come back home soon'

As Richard wheeled his war horse around and accompanied by Lovell who had just bade Bess a similar fond farewell, they rode towards London Bridge and the road to Dover.

When Richard reached Dover with the bulk of his army he found a hive of activity in progress as warships arrived to be victualled and made ready to transport the large body of men that were assembling to cross the Channel to Calais.

Meanwhile, he was kept busy receiving regular updates on the situation almost on a daily basis via his courier service from John who waited with almost the entire English garrison at Hammes Castle ready to try and halt the French advance fully aware that they were hopelessly outnumbered by the enemy. Three days after arriving in Dover and after conferring with his battle commanders, Richard, along with his trusted friends, Francis Lovell, Rob Percy, Richard Ratcliffe and William Catesby, embarked on his flagship, The Saint George, and led the flotilla with a stiff breeze behind them, speeding them on towards Calais which they reached in record time the following evening to be greeted with a rapturous welcome from the relieved townspeople led by the mayor and by John of Pontefract's deputy, Sir Thomas Stevens, whose orders were to defend the town to the last man if the worst happened and the French managed to break through the defences.

'What is the news from Hammes, Sir Thomas?' Richard asked tersely.

'Not good, your grace' He answered on bended knee.

'Sir John is heavily besieged and fast running out of arms and has lost many good men. The situation is desperate, your grace'

'Then we must make haste to relieve them' Replied Richard, at the same time summoning his commanders to a council of war inside the Captain of Calais's headquarters.

Seated at the head of a large table, Richard spread out a map of the area before him and pointing towards the northernmost edge of the Pale explained.

'The main body of our army will march up there then we will spread out and attack from the rear while you, Frank' He waved Lovell forward.

'Will make your way up to Hammes from here to relieve Sir John. That way we will surround the French and with God's help, we will annihilate them?'

'Aye aye'

Richard held up a hand for silence. 'We need to rest so away to your beds. We begin our march before daybreak tomorrow'

The breaking daylight on the following morning was heralded by the falling of heavy rain and a cold easterly wind which did nothing to lift the spirits as the army began the trek towards Hammes, their progress hampered by the churned up mud and puddles caused by the inclement weather as the foot soldiers dragged themselves and the horses pulling the supply wagons through the difficult terrain. Luckily, the rain had ceased by mid-morning when the scouts who had secretly gone on ahead reported back to Richard that the French were so busy besieging Hammes that they were unaware of the English advance and by the time that Richard's army arrived within striking distance, total pandemonium had broken out in the French ranks when they realised that they would be fighting a much larger on not one but two fronts as Francis Lovell and his men had arrived to come to the much needed aide of the sorely besieged Hammes garrison and as Richard, leading the main body of the English began to close in on them from the rear.

A tactic used successfully at sea during the Danish/French attempted invasion of Scotland. The ensuing battle was brief and brutal, the French overpowered by combination of Lovell's Bombards high on the castle's ramparts and by the constant hail of arrows let loose by the English Archers both behind and in front of them. This powerful combined onslaught decimated the French ranks whose few surviving foot soldiers attempted to flee, casting their weapons aside as they tried to escape the carnage around them. The mounted Knights fared no better being ruthlessly pursued by their English counterparts and cut down as they too attempted to escape. The entire battle had only lasted for just over two hours. Two hours in which much to Richard's surprise, his assistant secretary Thomas More, participating in his first battle had really distinguished himself fighting valiantly on foot after he had been unhorsed in the melee. His actions had not gone unnoticed by Richard so that immediately after the fighting ceased, he summoned More to his presence and bade him kneel before him as he drew his sword and knighted him saying,

'Arise, Sir Thomas More' And shook the unbelieving new knight by the hand.

Later that day inside the Castle of Hammes. Richard acknowledged the many congratulations from his Commanders as Lovell, watching his old friend closely, noted that he was looking somewhat pale and drawn and managing to take him aside asked.

'Are you well, Dickon. You look weary?'

'Aye, Frank, I am weary. God willing, this has been my last battle. I am getting too old for all of this'

'As we all are, Dickon,' Lovell nodded in agreement. 'As we all are'

Calais was saved. And it would be many years in the future before another attempt was made to oust England's only remaining foothold in mainland Europe.

# 41

The years following the saving of Calais were mainly peaceful except for minor uprisings in the Highlands between the warring clans and skirmishes on the wild Borderlands of England and Scotland that were quickly dealt with by the Wardens of the Marches appointed by both Richard and Mary respectively.

Their family continued to increase steadily with two more sons and a daughter born to James and to Catherine so the future succession was assured.

James was maturing into a steady younger version of his father with many of Richard's characteristics including his wry sense of humour. Richard created his second son, Richard the younger, Duke of York on the occasion of his marriage to Cecily, the beautiful daughter of Bess and Francis Lovell after obtaining a papal dispensation, necessary due to their close blood ties. Young Richard had grown into a handsome strapping young man who closely resembled his late uncle, King Edward IV in appearance with the same golden hair and impressive height but much to his parent's relief, without his uncle's promiscuous tendencies.

Inspired by the story of Christopher Columbus and his discovery of the American continent when he was a child, the younger Richard was filled with a burning ambition to follow in the footsteps of the famous explorer and to lead an expedition to discover more of the New World and to claim the unknown land for England. However, his hopes were dashed when his father refused his permission to finance such a venture.

'The time is not right,' Richard explained patiently to his downcast son.

'You are newly wed and how do you think your wife would feel if you deserted her so soon after your nuptials? And apart from that, you are needed here.'

The young duke bowed, accepting his father's judgement knowing that to argue any further would be pointless.

Of all his children, closest to Richard's heart, although he would only admit it to himself, was his daughter, Anne. And he was only too well aware that one day he would have to give her away in marriage and he dreaded the coming of that inevitable day which finally dawned in the September of 1505 when the sixteen year old Anne left Westminster to begin her long journey to Vienna to become the second wife of Maximilian, King of the Romans and Holy Roman Emperor. Anne had grown from being quite a tomboy as a child, always wanting to join her brothers in their rough and tumble games into the somewhat serious young woman that she had now become. While not conventionally beautiful, she possessed a wonderful warm smile that transformed her whole face so that everyone that she met never failed to be enchanted by her.

Richard fervently hoped that his darling daughter would have the same effect on her future husband when they finally met face to face. Politically, it was a splendid match that would raise her to the rank of Empress but the downside was that Maximilian at the age of forty six was thirty years her senior, a widower with a twenty seven year old married son, Philip.

Richard and Anne accompanied their daughter as far as Calais from where she would continue her overland journey to Vienna escorted by a large contingent of Austro/German nobles sent to welcome her to her new homelands on behalf of their emperor.

At last the day dreaded equally by Mary, Richard and the young bride arrived and it was time to say their final farewells. Anne was struggling not to break down and weep as Mary and Richard hugged her tightly for the last time as she prepared to enter her litter with its heavy silken curtains embroidered with the arms of England, Scotland and those of the Holy Roman Empire. They had said their private emotional farewells earlier when Richard had hung a golden Pendant with the White Rose of York picked out in Diamonds on both sides around her neck and when she flicked it open she found two miniature portraits of both her parents.

'Just so that you do not forget us,' he murmured kissing her forehead.

'Oh, I could never do that and I will always treasure this beautiful gift' she cried, hugging them both tightly.

'Be happy, my wee lass. I'm told that Maximilian is a kindly man,' Mary whispered in farewell.

The litter began to move slowly away as Mary grasped Richard's hand tightly. It had begun to rain but despite getting wet, they stood waving until the litter bearing their daughter away from them disappeared from their view and from their lives.

# 42

Anne was not the only loss that Richard sustained that year. His faithful old body servant, Tom Murgatroyd, now in his sixties, was finding it increasingly difficult to carry out his duties to his own high standards but he stubbornly refused to admit to himself that he was no longer capable of serving his king as he had been doing for over forty years.

His wife, Jeanie however told him in her customary forthright manner to 'Face facts, my lad. Ye canna carry on as you are, spilling water all over the floor and fumbling with his grace's clothing as you take ages these days to help him dress'

'Shut yer gob, woman. I have looked after his grace since he were a lad of ten and he don't complain so why should you?'

'Because I care about you, you daft old sod and I don't want you to work 'til you drop.' Jeanie shrugged before continuing, 'We could retire to that cottage in Middleham that your father left you. Yorkshire is no as good as Scotland but I could live with that.'

'Well, I couldn't,' he snapped, 'and that is the end of the matter.'

Tom dug his heels in and refused to discuss the matter any further but to his dismay, Richard brought up the subject one morning when Tom was taking much longer than usual to assist the king with his toilette.

'How old are you now, Tom?' he asked casually as Tom fumbled as he adjusted Richard's collar of sunnes and roses.

'I be sixty three,' Tom answered slowly as alarm bells began to sound inside his head.

'Ah yes, I remember now. You are ten years my senior.'

Richard glanced at Tom as he dropped his bed robe onto the rushes covering the floor with a muttered curse before folding it neatly and depositing it into a chest.

'Have you ever given any thought to retiring, Tom? I believe that you own a cottage in Middleham that would be ideal for taking life more easily in.'

Tom flushed a bright red as he struggled to think of a polite answer.

'Jeanie has mentioned it in passing, your grace,' he mumbled.

'And what was your reply?'

'Ah towd 'er I had many good years left in me yet, Sire.'

'I am sure that you have, but would it not be pleasant to have time to take your ease? And of course I would provide you with a decent annuity so you would have no money worries.'

'That's reet generous of you, your grace but—'

'Then that is settled, Tom,' Richard hastily interrupted. 'Can you think of anyone suitable that you could instruct in your duties?'

Conceding defeat, Tom replied, scratching his head slowly. 'I have a nephew who just might be suitable, Sire. With a little 'elp from me, that is.'

'Hmm, what is his name and where does he live?'

'His name is Jed Murgatroyd, Sire, and he lives in Ripon where he works as a Tailor.'

Richard tapped his top lip thoughtfully before continuing. 'Ripon eh, quite close to Middleham then. Tell me, why do you think he would consider giving all that up to enter my service?'

'Any man in his reet mind would be proud to serve your grace. But Jed is newly widowed, his wife snuffed it after a long illness and now he wants to get away from Ripon which he says has too many memories for him, and to make a fresh start somewhere else.'

'How old is your nephew, Tom?'

'He is about thirty, Sire.'

'And is he like you in his manner?'

'Nay, Sire,' grinned Tom. 'He is a bit on the quiet side, but not a misery guts if you get my meaning, your grace.'

'The good lord broke the mould when he made you, Tom,' laughed Richard. 'It would be impossible to have made two like you. I will see your nephew when we arrive in York next month.'

Two days following the arrival of the court in York, Tom presented his nephew to Richard after giving him a few words of advice beforehand. 'When we go in, don't forget to kneel. Don't stare at 'is grace and fer god's sake, lad, don't speak until you are spoken to. Have you got all that?'

'Aye, uncle,' he replied, nervously twisting his hat in his hands.

'Come on then, let's get it over with.'

Richard half expected to see a younger version of Tom but was surprised to see a tall thin young man with wispy shoulder length brown hair, neatly dressed and, he was pleased to note, with clean hands and nails, who had immediately dropped to his knees with his eyes modestly lowered on entering the King's presence.

'You must be Master Murgatroyd.' Richard spoke quietly, his hands resting before him on his desk as he looked him up and down.

'Yes, your grace,' Jed answered glancing up at the King.

Richard signalled for him to rise before continuing. 'Your uncle informs me that you may be interested in entering my service. Is that correct?'

'Yes, if it please your grace,' answered Jed with a quick glance upwards at Richard.

'I understand that for personal reasons you wish to leave Ripon and that you are willing to travel in my entourage?'

'That is true, your grace. I have no one left in Ripon now and I would be glad to put the past behind me.'

Richard nodded before asking, 'Are you a discreet man, Master Murgatroyd? As my body servant I must be able to rely on your discretion completely.'

'Certainly. Your grace can trust me to not indulge in idle gossip of any kind.'

Just then Prince, Richard's hound rose to his feet and sauntered across to Jed sniffing at him curiously before suddenly licking his hand. Jed reacted by tickling the large dog behind his ears.

'You seem to like dogs, Murgatroyd,' remarked Richard staring at him intently as the young man continued to stroke Prince.

'Aye, your grace. I do.'

Richard reached a decision. 'Very well, Murgatroyd. The position is yours on a three month trial in which your uncle will supervise your training. When can you begin?'

'I thank you, your grace. I can begin straight away as I have brought all my belongings with me.'

'Excellent. Your Christian name is Jed I believe?'

'Yes, your grace.'

'Well, Jed, in that case you can begin tomorrow and one of your first duties will be to give your new found friend, Prince here, a bath.'

'Well done, lad,' grinned Tom after they had bowed out of the royal presence. 'Play your cards reet and you will 'ave a job fer life'

The Court moved to Middleham for Christmas and when the celebrations ended so did Tom's long service. His nephew, Jed, had proved to be an excellent pupil and was now more than capable of attending to all his duties as the king's body servant and had earned Richard's approval in that capacity. The day that Tom and to a slightly lesser extent, Jeanie Murgatroyd, had been dreading arrived a week following Christmas at Middleham when Richard and Mary received their trusted servants privately, away from prying eyes to make their farewells and to present them with parting gifts after which Mary and Jeanie discreetly left the chamber leaving Richard and Tom alone.

'Well, Tom,' Richard spoke quietly. 'The time has finally come to thank you for taking care of me for so many years. I shall miss you, colourful language and all.'

'And I will miss you too, your grace,' gulped Tom, trying to hold his emotions in check. 'It has been a reet privilege for me to serve you, Sire, and thank ye fer putting up with me all this time.'

Then to Tom's amazement, Richard grasped his hand saying, 'You haven't seen the last of me, Tom. I will see you every time that I visit Middleham. Go now before I change my mind.'

# 43

The passing years were not uneventful for Richard. Apart from the usual minor skirmishes between the Highland clans and the Reivers on both sides of the English/Scottish borders that were quickly quelled. The two nations entered long periods of peace that enabled Richard to introduce new laws that brought more justice to the commons and slowly but surely eroded the powers of the lords ensuring that never again could there emerge another so called 'kingmaker'

Another act that would prove to have a long lasting effect on the security of his island kingdom was the founding of his regular Navy. Richard recognised the need to be on constant guard from potential threats of invasion from other European powers, especially from France and his navy provided a very effective deterrent.

In a concentrated effort to heal old wounds caused by the years of hostility between the rival houses of York and Lancaster, Richard and Mary regularly travelled the country. North to South, East to West to make themselves known to their people. The journeys were often arduous undertaken in inclement weather but the warmth of their welcome from the ordinary people, most of whom had never before laid eyes on a king or Queen, more than made up for their discomfort. They were especially touched during a visit to Devon when on an unseasonably raw day in October when they were passing through a small village on the edge of Dartmoor, an elderly couple shuffled forward from the crowd of curious onlookers and held out two well-worn woollen scarves for the sovereigns. Richard reined in his mount and Mary, following his lead, also halted.

'What have you got there, good master?' he asked quizzically.

'If it please you, your grace,' the old man replied in a quivering strong Devon burr. 'My wife thought that you and your lady Queen might feel chilled riding in the cold so she wondered if you would like these 'ere scarves to keep you warm.'

A cold glance from Richard quickly silenced the titters from their entourage before turning back to the elderly couple and holding out his hand he took one of the scarves with a smile and wound it around his neck as Mary accepted hers from the old lady.

'The Queen and I thank you, Master and Mistress for your kind gifts and bid you both good day'

The man and his wife bowed and curtseyed awkwardly as cheers and applause erupted from the bystanders as Richard and Mary continued on their way.

Another progress that took in visits to both Kent and Sussex, gave Richard the opportunity when staying in Ashford, for a rare meeting with his illegitimate son, Richard Broom, known locally as Richard of Eastwell, Respected Master Mason. Francis Lovell, acting in his long standing capacity as go between, arranged for father and son to meet privately at the Inn in Ashford where the royal party was staying for two nights.

The ideal opportunity arose on the first night when Mary, pleading a headache, retired early to her chamber which allowed Lovell to whisper, 'Master Richard Broom awaits you in my chamber, Dickon, where I will ensure that you will not be disturbed.'

Richard nodded and a few moments later entered the chamber as Lovell quietly closed the door behind him.

Father and son smiled awkwardly at each other before the younger Richard suddenly remembering his manners, hastily knelt only to be raised by his father saying, 'Stand up, lad. No need for any ceremony between us when we are alone.'

Ten years had elapsed since their last meeting. Ten years in which both father and son had wrought changes to both their appearances. The younger man at thirty eight sported a ruddy complexion from working outdoors in all weathers. Always stocky, he had put on weight and the only physical resemblance to his father was in his hands, the fingers of which were long and tapering but roughened with blackened and broken nails due to his trade as a Mason, while Richard at fifty six had retained his slim figure but now a few more lines had etched themselves onto his forehead and ran from his nose to his chin and his dark hair was lightly sprinkled with grey which Mary had kindly assured him, 'Made him look distinguished.'

'Viscount Lovell informs me that you have recently wed again, Richard. Allow me to congratulate you.'

'Thank you, Sire. Alice is a good woman and I am lucky to have her.'

Richard's eyes twinkled as he asked, 'And may I look forward to another grandchild in the future?'

His son laughed and red faced replied, 'I think that is highly unlikely, Sire. Alice is five years my senior and was a childless widow woman when we wed.'

'And does she know about me?'

'No, Sire. Alice is a simple woman and would be floored by such a revelation. She believes that the late Master and Mistress Broom were my real parents.'

'Perhaps that is as well,' Richard mused. 'So long as you are content then I am also.'

The short time together passed quickly as the younger Richard eagerly described his currant restoration work on the West Front of Canterbury Cathedral to his fascinated father until it was time for them to part. Richard hugged his son who in turn bowing, kissed his father's hand as they parted company.

Neither of them suspecting that they were destined never to meet again.

# 44

The beginning of the New Year 1512 was welcomed in as had become the custom for Richard and Mary and their family with the traditional Hogmanay celebrations in Scotland. This year held in the mighty royal fortress at Stirling at the start of what was to prove a significant year.

Once the winter snows had finally melted, Richard and Mary began a leisurely journey south with halts in Berwick, followed by Durham where Richard laid an offering from himself and from Mary, women not being allowed to approach it, at the shrine of St Cuthbert in Durham's majestic cathedral towering above the river Wear. Then it was on to Barnard Castle, one of Richard's favourite residences, before longer stays at both Middleham and at Sheriff Hutton. They arrived in York on a beautiful day in late April with the city ablaze with the Daffodils that grew in profusion on the mounds below the city walls, and to a rapturous welcome from the people of the city that Richard called home.

They lingered in York until mid-May before finally arriving at their journey's end in Westminster where soon after their arrival they received some long awaited news.

In the early summer of the previous year, Richard had bidden his second illegitimate son, Sir John of Pontefract, a reluctant farewell when he set sail from Tilbury to cross the almost uncharted Atlantic Ocean to explore the largely unknown Northern lands of the Americas first discovered by Christopher Columbus nineteen years previously in 1492. Many would be adventurers from all over Europe had since been inspired to follow Columbus's lead and to explore the vast new territories, including Richard's youngest son, the young duke of York. But it was Sir John of Pontefract who had finally obtained his father's consent to lead a fleet of eight ships into the unknown. Now, twelve months later, a flotilla of six badly battered ships had been seen entering the Thames estuary and slowly listing their way up river towards London.

As soon as the vessels had been recognised as those led by the king's son, messengers sped to Westminster to inform Richard that the fleet was in sight and slowly approaching Greenwich. Upon receiving word of his son's imminent arrival, Richard ordered the royal barge to be made ready immediately and accompanied by Mary, James and an excited young Richard, set sail down the Thames and arrived at Greenwich just as the first of the six ships made a shuddering landing at the pier. Richard and his family waited tensely while the gangplank was lowered on the first of the badly damaged vessels and to their relief, the first person to disembark was Sir John whose whole appearance had changed almost beyond recognition by the addition of a long straggly beard, a pronounced limp and his left arm supported by a sling. Despite all this, he attempted to kneel before his father but Richard quickly forestalled him by throwing an arm around his shoulder.

'Welcome home, lad. It is so good to see you,' he cried. 'Come away indoors and tell us what has befallen you.'

The family and their friends sat enthralled as John's great adventure unfolded, beginning with how he came by his injuries on the voyage back home.

'Our vessels have been battered by violent storms ever since leaving the New World, ' he began with a rueful smile. 'It was only through god's mercy that we lost no ships on our journey.'

Hearing this, the listeners crossed themselves and murmured, 'Amen to that.'

'But the lord took several of our men,' he sighed.

'How did you sustain your injuries, Sir John?' Mary asked the question that was on everyone's lips.

'It was about three weeks ago, your grace, in the face of a terrible storm. Our vessels were tossing about and we needed to lower the sails before they were torn to shreds by the winds. I was standing on deck instructing the men in their tasks when there was a loud creaking noise and one of the three masts snapped in half and crashed down pinning me to the deck. When I regained consciousness I was below deck being treated by our physician to whom I owe my life.'

174

'Pray introduce him to me at your earliest convenience, John,' Richard instructed. 'I wish to thank him for saving your life and will reward him.'

'Thank you, my lord father. He not only saved me but many of my men also. We would not have survived without his skill.'

At this point the duke of York could not contain himself any longer. 'Tell me, brother. Where did you finally make landfall in the New World?'

'Our supplies were running dangerously low when land hove into sight on the horizon. As we got closer we realised that the land the lookout had spotted was actually a small island and behind it a large tract of land that jutted out and on either side of which, separated by two rivers that ran into the ocean was more land. It formed a natural harbour so we dropped anchor beside the large piece of land in the centre.'

'And was the land inhabited by people?' Richard asked, listening intently.

'Aye, Sire,' John answered. 'But we did not see anyone until the following day when we were woken by loud voices speaking in a strange tongue.'

'Were these people friendly towards you?' Mary interrupted.

John smiled wryly before replying, 'It was very difficult to ascertain at first, your grace. They were as curious about us as we were about them.'

'What was their appearance like? Did they resemble us?' queried Richard.

John laughed before answering and shaking his head. 'No, my lord father. They are darker than us but not black like Africans and they dress very scantily in a curious loin cloth like garment with headdresses made from large coloured feathers.'

'Oh, John, how I wish that I had been there with you,' burst out young Richard before his father silenced him with a frown.

'We eventually managed to make closer contact by sign language,' John continued. 'We smiled, laid down our weapons and pointed to our mouths indicating that we were hungry and thirsty then the man in the largest headdress who seemed to be their leader, issued what appeared to be orders to half his men who scurried off into the forest behind them then he and the remaining men sat down

175

crossed their legs and signalled to us to join them which we did and before too long the men returned from the forest bearing strange food and clean water which they willingly shared with us'

'That is truly amazing,' exclaimed Richard. 'And what occurred next?'

'We got to know the tribesmen quite well and they even allowed us to see their women and invited us into their tent like homes.' John suddenly became serious. 'We owe them so much. We would surely have died from starvation without their help.'

Everyone fell momentarily silent as they absorbed this statement before John continued with, 'Well, after about two months when we had completed some essential repairs to our ships and taken aboard fresh provisions, we bade our new friends farewell and continued following within sight of the land that gradually became wilder and colder before making a brief landing on a deserted shore, I made the decision then that we should turn back the way we had come and try to make our way back home to England before the winter storms would made our voyage nigh impossible.'

'Mm, probably very wise.' said Richard thoughtfully. 'I could not help but notice that only six out of the eight vessels that set out have returned. What became of the others?'

'I am sorry, my lord father, they were too badly damaged to risk them attempting to cross the mighty ocean.'

'No need to apologise, lad,' murmured Richard. Then, with a change of mood he announced loudly.

'Come, everyone, we will eat now. And then you, lad, can tell us more about the New World.'

After John had told his fascinated audience more about his adventures, Richard asked him if he had given any thought for a name for the lands he had claimed for England.

'Two names sprang to my mind, lord father. If you approve, I would name our first landing place New York in honour of your royal house. And as the wild land further to the north reminded me of Scotland, I would like to name that in honour of her grace, our Queen,' he bowed to Mary who smiled graciously, 'as Nova Scotia.'

Richard and Mary caught each other's eye and grinned with mutual pleasure at John's suggestion.

'I think that I speak for both the Queen and for myself when we heartily approve of your excellent suggestions, my son,' said Richard as he rose from his chair and drawing his sword, commanded John to kneel before him, which he obeyed, not without some difficulty due to his injuries, as Richard tapping John's shoulders with his sword announced in ringing tones, 'Arise, Sir John. From this day onwards you will be known as Viscount Pontefract.'

# 45

On the second of October that same year, Richard's sixtieth birthday coincided with a visit by himself and Mary to Calais to inspect its defences and even more importantly for them on a personal level, to be able to meet their daughter, Anne, for the first time since her marriage to Maximilian, the Holy Roman Emperor, seven years earlier in 1505. The Imperial couple resided mainly in Vienna but important matters relating to their Burgundian lands had led to their temporary stay in Antwerp therefore making it possible for Anne to make the relatively short journey to be reunited with her parents in Calais.

The years of travelling on horseback around both his kingdom and that of his wife, together with the now ever constant pain in his back from the Scoliosis, was beginning to take its toll on Richard's health and much to his chagrin, he was now reliant on a stick for help with prolonged standing and for walking any distance. So when his daughter caught her first glimpse of his changed appearance her reaction was initially one of shock and dismay which she quickly disguised with a huge smile of welcome.

Anne had also changed from the shy sixteen year old princess whom her parents had last seen departing from Calais en route to her marriage in Vienna, into a self-assured and dignified young woman, very conscious of her rank as Empress of the vast Hapsburg Empire.

Richly arrayed in a gown of blue and white satin, heavily embroidered with Pearls, Sapphires and Emeralds in the shape of flowers and leaves and edged with Ermine, her floor length shimmering veil held in place by a large golden circlet studded with jewels, Anne made an imposing figure as she greeted her parents.

'I have so much to tell you,' she began. 'But first, my dear lord father and my lady mother, allow me to introduce you to your two grandchildren.'

Anne turned and nodded to her attendant who had accompanied her who then opened the chamber door and to Richard and Mary's delight, each holding a hand of their nurse, a small boy and girl entered.

'Oh, Anne, we did not expect to see these two beautiful children,' exclaimed Mary, kneeling with both her arms outstretched while Richard grinned from ear to ear.

Anne waved the Nurse aside, took her children's hands and brought them up close to her parents.

'Rudolph, Maria Anna, come and greet your lord grandfather and your lady grandmother.'

'God give you greetings, my lord and my lady,' lisped the children shyly, and to their grandparents' amazement, in perfect English.

Six year old Archduke Rudolph and his four year old sister bowed and curtseyed respectively before being swept up and kissed by both Mary and Richard and then seated on their knees where little Archduchess Maria Anna began to play with the gold chain that hung from Mary's neck which she immediately removed and placed over her granddaughter's head to squalls of delight, While Richard began to tickle his rather solemn grandson under his chin who soon relaxed and gave way to peals of laughter.

'I am both surprised and delighted that your children speak such excellent English, Anne,' Richard remarked later when his grandchildren were tucked up in bed and he and Mary got the opportunity to share some precious private time with their daughter.

'I always resolved it to be so, my lord father. So I spoke our language to them from their birth so that they have absorbed both English as well their native German.'

'A very commendable decision,' nodded Richard sagely.

'I am so sorry that this visit has to be such a short one,' said Anne, shrugging her shoulders apologetically. 'But, Maximilian wishes to return to Vienna without any further delay and of course, I and the children must return with him.'

'We understand, my dear,' replied Mary as Richard looked on downcast. 'But pray tell us. Are you happy in your marriage, and is Maximilian a good husband to you?'

'Yes, my lady mother. He is a good man and he asked me to give you both his good wishes and his sincere regrets that he is unable to meet with you on this occasion.'

Anne and her children said their tearful farewells the following day armed with gifts and messages of goodwill to her Imperial husband. Richard and Mary watched and waved to their daughter's cavalcade until it disappeared from sight, not knowing when or if, they would ever meet again.

Two days after Anne's departure, the King and Queen boarded their ship and embarked on their voyage back to England. They had decided to spend the coming winter at their palace in York where they would be joined by their two sons and their young families, so rather than make the short sea crossing from Calais to Dover and then the very long journey overland from Kent to Yorkshire, they concluded that it would be speedier, if the winds were right, to sail round the edge of England's south east coast and up into the North Sea and to enter the river Humber and make land at the town of Kingston – Upon - Hull in East Yorkshire followed by a relatively short journey onwards to York.

The fates were kind to them. There was a stiff wind behind their ship and the escorting vessels and on the fifth day after leaving Calais, they entered the Humber and landed as planned at the fishing port of Hull. Their ships had been noticed entering the river and the news had spread of their imminent arrival so that a large crowd had gathered on the quayside to welcome them home to Yorkshire.

From Hull the royal travellers and their company mounted their mettlesome horses, glad to be free at last from the confines of the ships, and rode to the nearby town of Beverley where they spent their first night ashore within the precincts of its majestic Minster.

There was heavy rain overnight but by morning it had cleared and gave the promise of a crisp, but sun filled day with the countryside ablaze with the autumnal colours of red and gold under a cloudless blue sky as a remounted Richard and Mary bade farewell to Beverley and led their cavalcade northwards towards York.

Their second overnight stop was in the small town of Pocklington, a mere fifteen miles from York.

The next morning they set off in high spirits after enjoying a hearty breakfast at the town's largest inn where most of the party had stayed overnight.

They were only five miles from York when suddenly they were struck by an unforeseen tragedy that would change Richard's life.

Mary and Richard were riding side by side at a steady pace and were laughing as they recalled an amusing incident involving Richard's personal servant, Jed Murgatroyd, when Mary's horse suddenly caught its hoof in a pothole, stumbled, and threw the Queen over its head and as she fell, striking her head on the deeply rutted road. The escorting riders immediately drew in their reins and shuddered to a halt and under the horrified gaze of the bystanders who lined the road hoping to catch a glimpse of their sovereigns as they rode by, watched as Richard hurriedly dismounted from his startled horse and limped to where his wife lay motionless on the ground.

'Marie, oh Marie, please speak to me,' he pleaded as with difficulty, he knelt beside her clasping one of her hands.

A few moments later he was vaguely aware of a hand pressing his shoulder and the familiar voice of his old friend, Rob Percy, who had accompanied them to Calais, saying softly with a sob, 'I am so sorry, Dickon, but your beloved queen cannot hear you because her neck is broken.'

'Dead, Dead from a fall from her horse? Rob. Her son, Robert died the same way. It cannot have happened for a second time.'

# 46

Richard gazed in horror at the angle at which Mary's head lolled and realised that Rob had spoken the truth as he felt the tears well up in his eyes which he quickly brushed away as Rob helped him to rise to his feet. A litter was brought forward from the rear, the seats were removed as Rob stooped again and carefully lifting Mary, placed her into Richard's outstretched arms taking care not to allow her head to droop

The now silent onlookers bowed their heads respectfully as Richard carried his wife slowly to the litter and refusing all offers of assistance, laid her gently on the cloak strewn floor, reverently folding her hands across her breast, he closed her eyes and gently kissed her badly gashed forehead before closing the curtains to find Rob mounted on his own horse and leading Richard's by the reins.

'Shall we be on our way now, Dickon?' he asked, sadly noting his old friend's dazed expression that struggled with the fact that Mary was gone from him forever.

Word had been sent ahead to York to alert the Mayor and the Aldermen of the city of the morning's tragic events, so it was to the mournful tolling of the bells from its churches that Richard, with his eyes cast down, rode beside the litter and past the silent townspeople who had gathered in the streets, until arriving at the palace gates.

Two weeks later, Mary's embalmed body lay in an ornate coffin before the High Altar in the palace chapel. Clad in her robes of state and a golden crown worn low over her forehead to hide her head wound and surrounded by four tall flickering candles that burned constantly both day and by night. Her internment had been delayed so that her two sons and their wives could make the journey from London to bid farewell to their mother and that the leading Scottish nobles and clergy led by the archbishop of St Andrews could pay their final respects to their Queen.

The day of Mary's interment dawned grey and wet with a heavy drizzle that quickly soaked through Richard's clothes and ran down his face and neck and those of all the mourners as they followed the coffin draped with Mary's personal standard and led by a lone piper, the short distance from the palace to the great west door of the Minster where the tolling of its heaviest bell replaced the sound made by the now silent piper.

On entering the Minster, the procession proceeded at a respectfully slow pace to the Chantry founded by Richard as a mausoleum for his family, and there, Mary was finally laid to rest.

The day following his wife's funeral, Richard stood before the summoned Anglo/Scottish Parliament and formally abdicated the Crown Matrimonial and watched with mixed pride and sadness as his eldest son, Prince James, was proclaimed king James V of Scotland and of the Isles by the earl of Angus as he knelt to receive a blessing from the archbishop of St Andrews.

All too soon, as it seemed to Richard, the time came for him to say farewell and Godspeed as James, Catherine and to their children as they prepared to leave for Scotland escorted by the Scottish delegation who had attended the late Queen's burial.

Richard warmly embraced his Spanish daughter - in -law of whom he had grown very fond of over the years since she first arrived in England as a demure young princess. Saying goodbye to his three grandsons and his little granddaughter was also very hard but hardest of all was parting from James who was in many ways, a mirror image of himself as a young man. Father and son looked into each other's eyes, they were of equal height, with their hands clasped. 'I will be praying for you on the day of your crowning, Jamie, and wishing that I could be there to see it.'

Misty eyed, Richard released James' hand to embrace him.

'I wish you could, my lord father. I only hope that one day, God willing, I will be able to follow in your footsteps and be as great a King as you are and that you will be proud of me' ' I am proud of you, my son, and always will be' Releasing him, Richard forced a laugh. 'And as for me being a great king. That *is* taking things a bit too far.'

'You still have me, my lord father' The duke of York interrupted, at the same time shaking his elder brother's hand in farewell.' I will always be here for you'

'I know you will, Richard. I am very fortunate indeed to have been blessed with two such wonderful sons,' his father said quietly.

# 47

The year following Mary's death and the departure of James for Scotland was not an easy time for Richard. He missed both his wife and son dreadfully but, there were some compensations. The country was experiencing a long period of peace in which Richard took the opportunity to introduce further new legislature which greatly benefited the commons while at the same time slowly, almost imperceptibly, eroding even more power from the nobles.

Richard spent his usual amount of time travelling around his realm between Westminster, the south and the midlands but he was happiest in his beloved north country and spent a month at the end of June at the place that held so many happy memories for him, Middleham, where he visited his old servant, Tom Murgatroyd who much to his dismay, he learned was now confined to his bed in his cottage in the town. Bedfast he may have been but Tom had lost none of his wit as he struggled to get out of bed to welcome his former master.

'Oh, Tom, stay where you are' Richard ordered placing a hand on his shoulder and gently pushing him back into bed.

'I'm reet sorry, your grace, that I can't greet proper like but it's my legs, they be a reet bugger.'

'Don't bother to apologise, Tom,' laughed Richard. 'I am just glad to see that you have not lost your unique way with words.'

For the next hour or so they chatted and recalled happy times past and then on a serious note, Tom said how sad he and his wife, Jeanie, were to hear about Mary's death.

'Me wife and me were reet sorry fer thee loss, Sire. Her grace was a gradely Queen and a lovely lady'

Richard nodded his thanks, too moved to reply.

Later, when they were alone together, Tom turned to Jeanie with a worried look. 'It were reet grand to see 'is grace again but 'e' worries me, lass, he don't look well and he is walking badly.'

'Alas, but we are all getting older, lad' Jeanie smilingly reassured her husband. 'It happens to us all ye ken.'

The 12 days of Christmas celebrations of 1513 drew to a close on a much happier note than those of the previous year. The court was in residence at Westminster. the winter so far, had been a particularly cold one which resulted in a hard frost that had caused the Thames to freeze over allowing for a staging of one of its famed Frost Fairs where traders sold hot food and drinks to the crowds of visitors who skimmed perilously across the ice on homemade skates made from pieces of animal bone tied round their boots.

The sound of music mingled with the laughter and shrieks from the fallen penetrated into the quiet chamber of the palace overlooking the river where Richard had just finished dictating a missive to Secretary Thomas More.

'Thank you, Thomas' Richard nodded. 'That will be all for today.' He strolled over to the casement as More collected the papers from off his desk and prepared to take his leave.

'Have you visited the fair, Thomas?' Richard turned and asked. 'The people seem to be enjoying it.'

'I plan to take my wife and children this evening, your grace.'

'I hope that you will all enjoy it,' Richard smiled wistfully.

'The music sounds quite good.'

Later that evening after dinner, Richard was joined around a roaring fire by a group of old friends that included Francis Lovell and his wife, Bess, Rob Percy, his wife, Joyce, plus Richard Ratcliffe and *his* wife, Agnes. But in prime position closest to the fire lay Richard's large Wolfhound, another descendant of Richard's beloved Rex. The gathering began to get livelier as the wine and ale flowed freely and reached the point where Bess decided that the time had come for the ladies to leave their menfolk to their reminiscences and no doubt bawdy talk.

She caught the eyes of the other ladies who nodded in agreement and they all rose to their feet as Bess curtseyed to Richard murmuring, 'With your permission, uncle, we ladies are feeling tired and crave your leave to depart.'

'Granted, if that is what you all desire,' Richard glanced at the curtseying ladies with a smile before turning to Bess and kissing her hand.

'God give you goodnight, my dear.'

Impulsively, Bess reached up and kissed his cheek. 'And goodnight to you too, uncle Richard.'

Richard stood thoughtfully watching as the chamber door closed behind Bess and the ladies until his reverie was interrupted by Francis Lovell. 'You seem to have gone quiet all of a sudden, Dickon, are you quite well?'

'Of course I am well, Frank.' He forced a laugh and slapped his old friend's arm playfully. 'Come, let us be seated and carry on where we left off before we were interrupted by the ladies.'

As the evening wore on the conversation turned to reminiscing about the past and to their days as young knights –to-be at Middleham.

'Those were happy days,' mused Lovell.

'Happy days until Warwick turned traitor and we had to make our choice,' put in Ratcliffe, frowning in remembrance of that difficult time when loyalties were tested to the utmost.

'There was only one choice possible for me,' Richard shifted uneasily in his chair, trying to ease the ache in his back that had troubled him more as the day had progressed. 'Warwick knew that I would always remain loyal to Ned who was not only my brother but also my King.'

'Aye.' They all nodded in agreement. Then taking advantage of the lull in conversation, Richard rose from his seat saying, 'The hour grows late, my friends, and it is time for me to seek my bed. I bid you all goodnight.'

'Goodnights' echoed round the chamber as the men, who had hastily risen to their feet, bowed as Richard clicked his fingers to his hound that lay with one eye open at his feet, who then leapt up and followed his master quietly through the open door.

Jed Murgatroyd was in the bedchamber waiting to help the king disrobe. ' I 'ave taken the liberty of putting three hot bricks in the bed instead of one, your grace, seeing as it is such a cold night,' he said, as Richard prepared to climb into bed.

'Thank you, Jed,' Richard replied. 'You have been a good servant to me, like your uncle before you.'

Jed flushed with pleasure at the unexpected compliment. 'I hope to 'ave the honour to serve your grace for many more years to come, Sire, God willing.'

# 48

Richard settled himself comfortably into his bed and soon felt himself drifting into sleep when suddenly he was wide awake, no longer in bed but outdoors in dazzlingly bright sunshine that blinded him momentarily but as his eyes adjusted themselves to the brightness he realised that he was not alone because Mary stood smiling beside him, and running towards him with arms outstretched in greeting, was his ten year old son, Edward of Middleham closely followed by his beloved first wife, Anne Neville, straining to hold a wildly excited Rex on a leash. Laughing happily, he began to run towards them, his back free from pain and with Mary following behind him.

The news of Richard's sudden death in his sleep at the age of sixty one devastated his family, his friends, and his people and on his final journey north prior to his internment in York Minster, led by his son, Richard, duke of York, as chief mourner, at every overnight stop, the local people turned out in their hundreds to pay their last respects to their king.

On their arrival in York on a bitterly cold day it was to find a city in mourning. The townspeople lining the streets crossed themselves as Richard's coffin, covered with his royal arms, passed them on its way to the Minster where it was met by the new king and Queen, James and Catherine, who had just arrived from Scotland and were clad in unrelieved black.

There followed a solemn Requiem Mass before Richard was finally laid to rest between his two former wives in the Chantry he had founded for this very purpose.

Immediately following the internment, on the steps of the Great West door of the Minster, trumpets sounded and a herald proclaimed in a loud voice.

'I give you king James V of Scotland and of the Isles who is by the death of our beloved sovereign lord King Richard III of blessed memory, now King James I of England and France. King of the United Kingdom of Great Britain.'

Thus began a new chapter in the history of the British Isles.

# Author's Note

Of course, this story of what followed after Richard III defeated Henry Tudor at the battle of Bosworth is pure fiction, but most of the principal characters are real. The exceptions being Tom and Jed Murgatroyd, Jeanie McColl and the children and grandchildren of Richard and Mary.

I have taken many liberties with the real people, necessary in the telling of this tale. Richard's friends and associates, William Catesby, Richard Ratcliffe, John Kendall, and Robert Percy all died fighting alongside Richard at Bosworth. It is not certain if Francis, Viscount Lovell actually fought at Bosworth, but he certainly fought beside Richard's nephew, John de la Pole, earl of Lincoln, who was killed in the last battle of the Wars of the Roses at Stoke, near Newark in 1487 in support of the pretender Lambert Simnel, which resulted in the final defeat of the Yorkists. Lovell escaped after the battle and then disappears from history. No proof of his ultimate fate has ever been found. Lovell certainly did not marry Elizabeth 'Bess' of York, the daughter of Edward IV and Elizabeth Woodville who married Henry Tudor and became Queen of England and mother of the Tudor Dynasty. Lovell actually wed Anne Fitzhugh daughter of Baron Henry Fitzhugh when they were both children in 1466.

Princess Mary Stewart was indeed the daughter of King James II of Scotland and his wife Mary of Guelders and the sister of King James III. Born on 13 May 1453 at Stirling, she died in 1488 aged only thirty five. She married twice. Her first husband being Thomas Boyd, first Earl of Arran, by whom she had two children, Margaret and James Boyd. Her second husband was James, the first lord Hamilton who was indeed almost forty years her senior. They went on to have three children, James, Elizabeth and Robert, Seigneur d' Aubigny who did not die young as in my story but lived to the age of sixty six, dying in 1543 at Torrence, Lanarkshire.

John Morton survived Richard's reign and was rewarded by Henry VII with the post of Archbishop of Canterbury on 6 October 1486. He went on to be appointed Lord Chancellor of England in 1487. He was created a Cardinal by Pope Alexander V1 in 1493. Morton became the mentor of the young Thomas More who served as a page in Morton's household. It is possible, but not proven, that Morton may have been the originator of Thomas More's History of King Richard III. John Morton died at Knole House in Kent on 15 September 1500 and was buried in the crypt of Canterbury Cathedral.

Margaret Beaufort and her son, Henry Tudor, both died in 1509 and are buried quite close to each other in magnificent tombs in Westminster Abbey.

King James IV of Scotland went on to marry Margaret Tudor, eldest daughter of Henry VII and Elizabeth of York. He actually died fighting against the English at the battle of Flodden in Northumberland on the 9 September 1513 aged forty and became the last monarch to die in battle in Britain.

Richard's nephew, Edward, the childlike earl of Warwick, was imprisoned in the Tower of London by Henry Tudor and executed on a trumped up charge in 1499 at the age of twenty four. His sister, Margaret, did not take the veil as in this story but was married to Sir Richard Pole, a cousin of Henry Tudor in 1487 and went on to give birth to five children including Reginald, Cardinal Pole who eventually became the last Roman Catholic Archbishop of Canterbury. Margaret's ultimate fate was to be beheaded in the Tower in a particularly brutal fashion in 1541 at the age of sixty seven on the orders of Henry VIII who zealously carried on his father's policy of eradicating any Yorkist threats to the Tudor Dynasty.

John of Pontefract or, as he is sometimes known, John of Gloucester, did not embark on a voyage of discovery to the New World, but was appointed Captain of Calais by his father, King Richard, and was serving in that capacity at the time of the battle of Bosworth. He was removed from his post by Henry VII. He died in 1499, probably executed.

In this novel I have made Richard of Eastwell an illegitimate son of Richard III. But despite many theories, his true identity remains unknown.

History is full of 'What if's.' This novel is about just one of them.

31465449R00109

Printed in Great Britain
by Amazon